Love on the Brain

a short fiction collection

Delaney Diamond

Garden Avenue Press

Contents

A Taxicab Connection

Prince Kofi

Thirty Minutes

Happily Ever After in Hopevale

A Taxicab Connection

Synopsis

Immediately after a painful break up, Erica meets a man who makes her feel much better. Could he be her next love?

Chapter One

She was done.

After hiding in the bathroom for five minutes, Erica rushed out of the restaurant without saying goodbye to Simon. Tears burned the back of her eyes, but she hurried down the stairs and waved her arm wildly to capture the attention of the yellow cab coming her way. The driver pulled to a sudden stop in front of Bella Blu, a high-end establishment with a prix fixe menu and a waiting list two months long.

"Erica, wait!"

Simon's voice came loud and clear behind her as she yanked open the cab's back door. She quickly climbed in.

"Go, go!" she begged, voice quivering.

She didn't turn in the direction of the restaurant, but she did hear Simon yell her name one more time as the vehicle pulled away from the entrance.

"Where to, ma'am?"

She gave the driver her address. Once he had gone a full mile, the tension oozed from her body, and she relaxed into the leather seats and gazed at the passing night time scenery.

It was over. Two years down the drain.

"Are you okay?"

His warm, low voice caught her attention. Concerned eyes met hers in the rearview mirror. Eyes that momentarily stunned her with their liquid brown beauty.

"Yes," she answered.

Then, as if the question had broken through her protective shell, her bottom lip trembled, and her eyes filled with tears. Those tears overflowed onto her cheeks, and she angrily wiped them away. Humiliated, she sniffled and kept her gaze lowered.

"Here you go."

The softly spoken words were followed by a tiny box of tissues that appeared in front of her. Her eyes met the driver's in the mirror again.

Erica took the box. "Thank you," she said in a hoarse voice.

She removed several tissues, dabbed her eyes, and blew her nose.

After a few minutes, the driver cleared his throat. "Want to talk about it?"

She stared at her lap. "Not really."

He didn't respond, and the silence suddenly seemed louder and untenable. He was being kind, and his kindness nudged her to share, to get the weight of the night's trauma off her chest. "I ended a relationship."

"Male or female?"

"Male."

"What did he do?" he asked in a resigned voice.

That prompted a smile, albeit a very small one, from Erica. "How do you know it was his fault?"

"Am I wrong?"

"No." She swallowed the painful lump in her throat and continued. "Tonight was our two-year dating anniversary. He's been out of town for two weeks on business, so he said. Right before our dinner date, I received a call from a woman who said she's been having a relationship with him for the past six months. She lives in Cincinnati, where he's been traveling to for work."

"Damn. But why did you go to dinner with him if you knew about the other woman?"

"I guess... I don't know. I didn't want to believe it. Hoped it wasn't true. Silly, I know."

"I don't think that's silly. I think that's pretty normal. What did he say?"

"Denied it. Then I showed him the screenshots of texts she sent me."

They had both sent explicit messages about what they wanted to do to each other when they were apart, as well as recalling the tawdry details of their sexual exploits when they were together. Equally hurtful were the messages Simon sent complaining that he wasn't happy and how much he missed the other woman.

"What did he say when you showed him the texts?"

Erica released a little laugh. "He still denied the relationship, but he has a tell. Whenever he lies, his nostrils flare. They flared a lot during our conversation."

"Sorry to hear that."

He couldn't be more sorry than she was. She had been devastated.

She took a good look at her driver. He seemed around her age, early thirties. Dark copper skin, and those beautiful brown eyes. With a trimmed beard and a deep voice, he was kind of attractive. He wore a black hoodie and had large hands with long fingers gripping the wheel, but she couldn't see much more than that from the backseat.

"Do you have a girlfriend?" she asked, shocking herself that she asked such a question. Hopefully, he didn't consider it inappropriate.

He shook his head. "Nah. Haven't had a girlfriend in over a year."

Surprising. Since he apparently didn't mind the question, she continued to get up in his business. "Why not?"

They bounced over a pothole, and Erica gripped the door as the cab swerved.

"Sorry about that."

"That's okay." Erica straightened her skirt and crossed her legs.

"I broke up with my last girlfriend because her parents didn't approve of us. She's wealthy, and I made a bad financial decision a few years ago, so money is kinda short."

"You have to explain that. What happened?"

"I'll give you the condensed version. I went into business with a so-called friend. His credit was jacked up, so I signed all the loan documents because I had good credit. When the business fell off, he left me high and dry. I *thought* we were in it together, but apparently not. Since my name is on all the paperwork, I was left with all the debt for a business that no longer exists, and now I'm stuck driving taxis part-time to pay off the loans and maxed out credit cards."

"That's terrible." She could never understand how people could be so cruel. "So you were trying to be an entrepreneur."

He nodded. "I believe we could have turned the business around if my friend had stuck with me through the difficult period. I explained to him that a lot of businesses don't turn a profit in the first year or so, but he wouldn't listen. Guess he was looking for quick money. Anyway, because I was struggling financially, I told my girl to move on. I can't support the lifestyle she's used to, and her parents were threatening to cut her off because I'm not exactly the kind of man they had in mind for her."

"Did you love her?"

"Yeah."

"But not as much as you should," Erica guessed.

Their eyes met in the rearview mirror again.

"No," he answered honestly.

The cab fell into silence. The roadway was busy on a Friday night, but not too busy. Looking at the cars and buildings passing by filled her with sadness. She should be sitting at Bella Blu, finishing her lobster and scallop dinner with a glass of champagne, while celebrating two years with the man she loved. Instead, she was prematurely on her way home, heartbroken and wondering what to do next.

Chapter Two

Erica's phone vibrated, and she removed it from her purse. A missed call from Simon. And she'd missed two texts from him, apparently.

Text one: *I know you don't want to talk to me right now, but when you calm down I can explain.*

Text two: *It was a mistake. She meant nothing to me.*

There it was, an admission of guilt. Erica pressed her lips' together, fighting the ache in her chest. At least he was no longer denying the affair. She assumed she and Simon would eventually marry, but clearly that was not the case. She could never trust him again.

Another message popped up on the screen. *Please answer. We need to talk.*

Erica powered off the phone and slipped it into her purse. "Do you mind making a small detour?" she asked the driver.

"Not at all. I'm on your time."

"Get off at the next exit and make a left at the fork. There's a doughnut shop on Eighth Avenue. It should still be open."

"Oh yeah, I know the one you're talking about. Donut

Parlor. It's open. On Fridays and Saturdays they stay open until ten."

She smiled, oddly pleased he knew about the shop. "They have the best cake doughnuts," she said.

"Yeah, they do. Don't sleep on their glazed, though. You know which one is my favorite?"

"Which one?"

"The Nutella with Oreo cookie sprinkles."

"Oh my goodness, they are the *best*."

He chuckled at her breathless enthusiasm. "No doubt. Have you ever had their breakfast? The sausage, egg, and cheese biscuits are freaking delicious. The biscuits are so flaky, and they use two eggs, so it's very filling."

"No, I haven't. I'm not usually on this side of town, but based on your recommendation I'll have to make a special trip one day."

"You won't be disappointed, trust me."

Minutes later, he pulled in front of the shop, and Erica went inside. She placed her order and returned to the taxi with a box of six doughnuts.

As they pulled away, she bit into a cake doughnut and let out a soft moan. There were few problems in life a box of freshly made doughnuts couldn't fix. For the moment, she looked past her devastating night and enjoyed the simple pleasure.

Scooting forward, she held the open box over the front seat. "Want one?"

He glanced at the box but shook his head. "No, I'm good."

"You sure? The Nutella with Oreo cookie sprinkles has your name on it."

He groaned. "Now why did you do that? I'm watching my figure."

Erica giggled. "It's okay to cheat just this once. You can make it up tomorrow."

"I like the way you think."

He took the doughnut, and she handed him a napkin.

"Thanks."

"You're welcome."

They spent the rest of the ride in easy conversation, and she learned he repaired computers in his day job. She shared that she taught third grade and came from a family of teachers.

They ate another doughnut each, and a few times he made her laugh out loud. When he pulled in front of her house, she felt a little sad, as if she was about to be separated from a good friend.

That's when she realized she didn't know his name. Her gaze found his posted identification. Robert. The name fit him.

"How much do I owe you?"

"Twenty dollars and nineteen cents."

Erica frowned, certain he was wrong. She checked the meter. "We drove much more than that."

"I turned off the meter when you went into the doughnut shop."

Her lips parted in surprise. "Why?"

Robert shrugged. "Guess I was enjoying the company."

The words warmed her heart but also sent a small thrill through her bloodstream. Was she attracted to this guy? Definitely. But maybe it was too soon to be thinking in those terms. She had broken up with her boyfriend less than an hour ago.

She handed Robert a twenty and a ten. "Keep the change."

He turned in the seat. "No. Come on..."

"I enjoyed the company too. You made a bad night better. Have a good one."

Erica climbed out the vehicle and walked to the front door of her townhouse. Once inside, the taxi pulled away from the curb. She flipped on the lights and kicked off her heels. Placing the doughnuts on the counter, she realized with a start that she was smiling. Despite the painful dinner and the revelation that the man she loved had been cheating on her for at least six months, she ended the night in a good mood.

She transferred the doughnuts to a container and poured herself a glass of wine. Strolling barefoot into the living room, she stopped in front of a photo of her and Simon on the fireplace mantle. A bout of nostalgia hit her in the chest. Her lower lip trembled, but she quickly shoved off the desire to cry.

She knew the truth now, and eventually she would get over him.

She turned the frame face down and took a gulp of wine.

Tomorrow she would pack up his belongings and leave them on the porch for him to pick up. She never wanted to see or talk to Simon again.

The doorbell rang.

Erica frowned. That better not be Simon. If so, she would give him a piece of her mind.

She set down the glass of wine and marched to the door. Peering out the peephole, she drew a sharp breath when she saw Robert standing outside.

She opened the door. "Hi. Did I forget something in the car?"

As far as she could remember, she had her purse, phone, and the doughnuts.

Looking at him head-on, she was struck even more by the beauty of his eyes. But not only that, he had great posture and a muscular build beneath the hoodie and jeans. About six feet tall, his height would require her to raise up on tiptoe if she wanted a taste of his very attractive mouth.

Heat filled her cheeks. Where did that thought come from?

"No, you didn't. I came back because I figured since we

both enjoyed each other's company, and I found you really easy to talk to, then..." He extended a white business card.

Erica took it.

"That's my card with my cell number. I'd like to take you out sometime. I can't afford Bella Blu at the moment, but I can take you to a more moderately priced place, and on the nights we don't go out, I grill a mean steak. So, whenever you're ready to start dating again, call me."

Erica couldn't suppress the wide grin that overtook her face. "I will."

His face broke into a full grin too. "I'll be waiting."

Oh my.

Robert walked away.

"Robert!"

He paused halfway to the cab.

"My name is Erica." She sounded breathless, her heart rate kicking up a notch.

He stuffed his hands in his pockets. "Like I said, I'll be waiting, Erica."

She watched him climb into the taxi and drive away.

Walking into the living room, her attention locked on the card in her hand.

Who knows... he might not have to wait too long.

Prince Kofi

Synopsis

Before *Princess of Zamibia*, Prince Kofi Karunzika traveled to the United States and fell in love with Dahlia Sommers. The woman who would capture his heart, become his bride, and become the mother of his heirs.

Chapter One

Crown Prince Kofi Francois Karunzika, Conquering Lion of the tribe of Mbutu, heir to the throne of the West African nation of Zamibia, stepped down from the black chauffeur-driven SUV onto the dark pavement of the parking lot. His second day in the United States had landed him at Wane Property Management in New York to check on the buildings his parents had purchased. His four-man security detail alighted from the dark sedan behind him, but he signaled with a wave that they should remain at the vehicle instead of following him inside. Kemal, his assistant, came around from the other side of the vehicle.

"What's the final word on Miss Wane?" Kofi asked.

Kemal was a tall man with licorice-colored skin and a strip of blue-dyed hair running down the middle of his head, a decorative flourish unique to his tribe. Like Kofi, he wore a suit and black shoes polished to a shine. He had just gotten off the phone with Melanie Wane, the owner of the management company.

"She had an emergency at another building and won't be able to meet and show us the properties, so she's asked her partner to handle the showings in her absence."

Kofi's lips firmed in displeasure. He preferred to work with the person he'd been in communication with, but he'd arrived a day early and they were accommodating his change of plans. He hoped the partner was as knowledgeable and capable of answering questions.

He didn't often visit the United States, but an increase in maintenance and repairs prompted his father to send him to inspect their real estate portfolio and handle renovations. The buildings needed to generate adequate revenue because they were used to finance university scholarships for deserving Zambian students who wanted to study in the U.S.

The one thing he appreciated about the United States was that no one knew who he was. He could keep a low profile, despite the bodyguards and assistant. He was not a celebrity or TV personality. His father was aging, and as the heir to the throne, Kofi had to be protected at all times. The stability of his nation depended on it.

"What's his name?" he asked Kemal.

"*Her* name is Dahlia Sommers. She's waiting for us inside."

"Let's meet Miss Sommers and get started. Maybe we can wrap up the visit early enough to grab a show."

The corners of Kemal's mouth twitched but didn't quite make their way into a smile. He knew Kofi was referring to a burlesque show a friend had spoken highly about.

"Your Highness, if you're photographed in one of those places..." he warned.

Kofi grinned and clapped his assistant on the shoulder. "I'm doing it for the men. They work hard and deserve some down time," he said, tongue in cheek.

"Oh, it's for the men. In that case, you're quite generous," Kemal said.

Kofi laughed softly as they walked toward the front of the building.

Chapter Two

C*rap.*

With trembling fingers, Dahlia struggled to pin up her hair before her appointment arrived. The thick, wavy mass had already stretched and broken a rubber band, so she improvised with a ribbon she'd found in the supply closet.

Unfortunately, Melanie was stuck on the other end of town dealing with an emergency at another building. Since Dahlia was the next senior person, she needed to handle the meeting with the prince—a meeting she was not prepared for.

The Karunzika family was their biggest client. And royalty! No one from the royal family had ever visited the office. They usually used a third person to handle communication and transactions.

She shoved a second paperclip into her hair to create a neat ball at the back of her head. A knock sounded on the bathroom door, and the receptionist, Lola, peeked in. Long bangs and straight, blunt-cut hair that landed on her shoulders, framed her face.

"Please tell me you're ready," she said in a hushed, panicked whisper. She shoved a pair of glasses higher on her nose.

"Why?" Dahlia paused in the midst of sticking another paperclip into her hair.

"Because I let him into the office a minute ago. He's sitting on the sofa out front, waiting."

Dahlia cursed under her breath and finished securing her hair. Then she dropped her hands and faced Lola. "What do you think? This is the best I could do on such short notice."

"You look fine," Lola said.

Dahlia took another quick glance in the mirror to assess her appearance. The office had a fairly relaxed dress code. While the crossover maxi was fine any other day, she wished she'd worn more professional attire. Well, it wasn't her fault. She'd had no idea when she dressed this morning she would be meeting their most important client.

"Okay, this is it." She took a deep breath.

"By the way, he's fine as hell," Lola said out the corner of her mouth, as if someone else were in the vicinity to overhear them.

Dahlia rolled her eyes. "Not now."

"What? I'm just saying..." Lola shrugged. She constantly checked out men who entered the building. She married young and after her divorce decided to take a new lease on life, which meant dating often and without discrimination.

"Give me five minutes and then send them in."

Lola nodded and hurried off, and Dahlia rushed down the hall to the newly expanded office space, which included two additional offices for their growing team of managers.

She entered Melanie's inner sanctum and swept her gaze over the room to make sure nothing was out of place.

Over the past year, the business had grown exponentially

and Melanie completed extensive renovations and redecorated. Her private office was larger than Dahlia's, with heavy leather furniture and dark wood dominating the decor. On one end, the seating arrangement for guests included a leather sofa and two leather armchairs around a heavy wood table. For Dahlia's tastes, the room was a bit much, and the new chairs not nearly as comfortable as the soft, cushy ones tossed out during the redesign. But Melanie's office was more impressive-looking than hers, which contained colorful furnishings and walls filled with framed photos that displayed her photography hobby.

Dahlia printed the property details and retrieved them from the nearby printer within seconds of Lola leading two men into the office. She straightened her spine and settled a smile on her face.

Right away she knew which one was Prince Kofi because, well, he looked like a prince. He stood behind the first man and had a presence about him that drew the eye. He was impressively tall and wore a dark suit that fit snug over his broad shoulders and torso.

Her eyes lingered on him. Lola was right. He was definitely fine as hell, with mahogany skin and a well-groomed circle beard that brought attention to his full lips.

"Good afternoon, I am Kemal, assistant to Prince Kofi Karunzika, His Royal Highness of the Kingdom of Zamibia."

Dahlia's gaze snapped to the man in front of her, and her face heated with embarrassment as she realized she'd been staring at the prince. "Good afternoon, Kemal. I'm Dahlia Sommers, Melanie's partner." She stuck out her hand.

Slender and smartly dressed in a dark suit, he didn't return her smile. Her shoulders tightened slightly as his bony fingers crushed her hand, but she refrained from wincing.

"Allow me to also introduce Prince Kofi Karunzika."

Dahlia's gaze shifted to the prince, who nodded politely but didn't say a word or extend his hand. Perhaps he didn't speak English.

Unsure if she should address him, she didn't. "Melanie is very sorry she couldn't be here to meet you, but I'm familiar with the properties and can take you to wherever you need to go." She held up the sheets of paper she'd printed.

"Good. Then we can get started," Kemal said.

"Can I get you both anything to drink? Coffee? Water?" Dahlia asked.

"We're fine."

"Please, have a seat." She gestured to the uncomfortable chairs that flanked the low table. "So, have you been in the States long?"

"No."

"I see." Okay, so much for building a rapport. Dahlia shifted on the chair opposite them. "Let's get started with the properties. As I understand it, you'd like to take a look at Emerald Estates and one in Brooklyn. Is that correct?"

"We'd like to take a look at all of them."

"All of them?" Dahlia asked, unable to keep the alarm out of her voice. There were seven in all, spread out across the city, and Melanie had only mentioned those two.

"Is that a problem?" Kemal asked.

"Not a problem...exactly. But we should have started earlier, if that's the case. These visits will take some time."

Kemal leaned forward, eyebrows snapped together as if she'd said something inappropriate. "So showing us the properties *is* a problem?" he asked with an imperial tone to his voice.

Kofi placed a hand on Kemal's shoulder, and the other man sat back in the chair. Without saying a word, he'd given a command and had it immediately obeyed. "What Kemal is asking, is how much of your time do we have today?"

He spoke! In English. Good heavens, he had a rich, attention-getting voice. Intoxicatingly deep and so smooth that her breath hitched at the sound of it. He also spoke with an accent, but for some reason his was sexier and laden with more sensuality than Kemal's.

Dahlia drew in a silent breath and gave him her undivided attention. "My understanding is that you want to inspect the properties, but this late in the day we'll be at the mercy of nightfall in a couple of hours, which makes it hard to do a proper inspection of the exterior and grounds, if you're interested in doing that."

"Because of their distance from each other?"

"Yes."

"I see."

Kofi conversed with his assistant in another language, and Dahlia stared at his regal profile before catching herself and lowering her gaze to the sheets on her lap. Her internal temperature rose as she listened to him speak. She'd never been so turned on by a voice before.

"Miss Sommers, how many properties did you have on the schedule today?" Kofi's dark gaze rested on her face.

"Two," Dahlia replied.

"Then we are ready when you are," the prince said.

A faint smile touched the corners of his mouth, and Dahlia couldn't help but smile back, even as butterflies danced in her belly.

"In that case, shall we be on our way?"

Chapter Three

From the moment they met in her office, Kofi found it difficult to pry his eyes away from Dahlia. Not only because she was exquisite to look at, but he'd liked her immediately, drawn to her friendly, dark brown eyes.

She walked ahead of them in one of the empty units, pointing out repairs completed after the last tenants moved out.

While he'd expected someone older, more serious, and dressed conservatively in a suit, his gaze lingered in appreciation on her shapely backside beneath the light-colored dress, belted at the waist. The V-neckline didn't dip low enough to expose her breasts, but did pique his interest at her curvaceous figure. She pointed out the upgraded kitchen with fingers adorned with stacked silver rings on her thumb and forefinger, her style suggesting an easy-going personality—breezy, casual, relaxed.

"What do you think?" She held a leather-bound pad against her chest and looked at him expectantly.

For a moment, Kofi couldn't answer, distracted by the beauty of her dark-sepia skin and wavy hair that barely stayed contained. Although she wore it in a bun, strands of the shiny black mass escaped confinement and trailed down her back, tempting him to swipe them back into place.

He strolled over to the window and looked at the almost full parking lot. "Very nice. How soon do you think you'll have someone to move in?" Their intermediary collected this type of information, but he asked anyway, stalling. Kemal hovered behind her, silent and watchful.

"We're working on that now. These units don't stay empty long once we've turned them. We have a couple of applications already and are waiting on the work verification to come back on the first one."

Kofi ambled over to where she stood. "Good. And the roof? I understand it was replaced recently?"

Dahlia frowned. "On this building? No, that's not right."

Kofi flicked his gaze to Kemal, who took a step forward. "That is correct, Your Highness."

"No, that's not correct," Dahlia insisted. "We had the roof of one of the buildings on the Golden Estates property replaced —oh, about six months ago. Maybe that's the one you're thinking about?" She glanced between them.

Kofi flicked his gaze to Kemal again.

"I will look into it," Kemal said.

"So will I." Dahlia flipped open the pad and wrote a quick note. "Well, you've seen both properties, and as I mentioned, it's already getting dark. When is the next time you're available? I can pull together the information on the others. I checked Melanie's schedule before we left, and she can take you out as early as ten in the morning."

Kofi frowned. "You won't be the one showing us the other properties?"

She smiled politely. "No. I don't usually handle this aspect of the business. My tasks center around PR and marketing. If you'd like to start earlier in the day, we could arrange for a property manager to escort you. One of them should be free tomorrow."

"And what if I want to remain in your excellent hands?" Kofi asked.

Her eyes widened slightly at that question, and he watched the movement of a slow swallow in her throat. "Oh...well." She laughed, appearing flustered. "Like I said, I don't normally do this, and I'm sure Melanie would prefer to take care of you herself, or assign your care to someone else."

"We started with you and want to end with you. Are you saying you're not up to the task?"

"I'm up to the task," she said, angling her head a little higher.

"Then I believe it's settled. You will be our escort for the rest of the trip. Are you available tomorrow?"

"No, I have a full day tomorrow."

Kofi knew from past experience that persistence would get him his way. He could think of very few times he had ever been refused anything he requested.

Locking his gaze with hers, Kofi came to stand directly in front of her, only an arm's length away. The couple of hours he'd already spent in her company increased the initial spark he experienced at their introduction in the real estate office. As he looked down at her, he recognized his fascination was not one-sided. The gravitational pull between them manifested in the dilation of her pupils and the way her full, moist lips remained parted as she breathed through her mouth. He wanted to touch her. He wanted to see if her skin was as soft and supple as it appeared. He wanted to push his fingers into her thick hair and claim her mouth.

"Are you available the day after tomorrow?"

"No. I am the day after that, but I should really talk to Melanie about this," she said softly.

They both gazed at each other, and he momentarily forgot they weren't alone. Kemal stood nearby, but for the life of him, Kofi couldn't bring himself to break his attention from this woman.

"Kemal will talk to Melanie on my behalf and explain you are the one I want to work with moving forward." He gestured at the door. "After you."

Dahlia tore her gaze away and walked ahead of him out of the unit.

His gaze dropped once again to her curvaceous form, and he made up his mind that there would be more than business between them. Dahlia would be his last hurrah before he went home and gave in to his responsibilities.

Chapter Four

He touched her on purpose. There was absolutely no doubt in Dahlia's mind.

The hallway of the unit they inspected was wide enough to accommodate them both, yet when she stood aside for Kofi to enter the bedroom ahead of her, his hand brushed her wrist. Contact had only been in one small spot, but heated awareness engulfed her skin and spread up her entire arm.

She clutched the leatherbound pad to her chest and followed him into the room, more aware of him than she'd been when they met three days ago. This time she noticed other details about his features. He appeared a little older than her, perhaps in his late twenties but exuding the solemn maturity of someone much older. Thick eyebrows and enviously high cheekbones rounded out the perfection of his face, which no doubt had convinced many women to succumb to him in the past.

It didn't help that he called several times during those few days, refusing to speak to anyone else but her. Their conversations didn't center on the properties. He slipped in personal questions. Despite her better judgment, she willingly answered.

Do you have any siblings? No, I'm an only child.

Do your parents live in New York? No, they passed away in a car accident.

What do you do in your spare time? I enjoy photography. Mostly black and white photos.

Shifting her focus from his appearance, Dahlia scanned the interior of the room. The corner apartment was located approximately ten minutes from NYU. The white palette worked well with the blond hardwood floors and allowed for plenty of imagination when decorating.

Kofi's gaze flicked across the ceiling fan. "So far so good. Modern kitchen, very clean, close to the university." He nodded to himself.

"We do our best to maintain the properties in tip top condition," Dahlia said.

His dark gaze returned to her, and once again instant attraction crackled across the small space that separated them.

He certainly made it hard to ignore him, especially today. She'd been surprised when he told Kemal to wait in the SUV with the driver. This was the last building on the list, and she still hadn't gotten used to being alone with him. She noticed every move he made, and her skin prickled each time he looked at her. She wanted to make small talk but felt out of sorts. She'd never been so overwhelmed in a man's presence before.

"You do a good job," Kofi said slowly.

"Thank you," Dahlia said.

Next, she led the way to the living room and opened the sliding glass door to show off the small balcony staged with patio furniture.

His examination continued in silence, his keen gaze missing nothing. They stepped back inside.

Dahlia closed the glass door. "What do you think?"

"This property seems to be in good condition, like the others."

"You were expecting something else?"

He didn't answer, instead running his palm across the bar that separated the kitchen from the living room. "You said this was the last one, yes?"

"Yes." She nodded.

"Good. Then I'd like to take you to dinner."

"Excuse me?" She let out a surprised laugh.

"I think you should have dinner with me."

She laughed shakily. "Just like that?"

He smiled. "Yes, just like that."

She'd sensed the burgeoning attraction between them, but to have him confirm was almost too good to be true. Still, it was better to proceed with caution, especially since she was way too excited, her rapidly beating heart threatening to burst from her chest. And, of course, he was a client.

"I don't mix business and pleasure, Your Highness. I don't think going to dinner with you is a good idea."

A small smile crossed his lips. "Why not? We're going to celebrate that my inspection has shown Wane Management is taking very good care of our properties. Or would you prefer that I ask you on a date?" His gaze dropped temporarily to her left hand. "You're not wearing a ring, so you're probably not married. Do you have a boyfriend?"

She hesitated.

"Please don't lie."

She released a sigh of resignation. "No, I don't."

"Then you're free."

"You're being rather presumptuous, aren't you? Assuming I'd want to?" Dahlia straightened her spine.

A smile came to his lips. "Are you saying you don't? I'd like to take you out to dinner and get to know you better. Would you do me the honor of allowing me to take you out?"

"I guess you expect my answer to be yes."

"Expect it? Why?"

"Because you sit on a gold throne and run a country."

"Well, it does usually impress women."

Despite herself, she laughed and then shook her head. "I'm afraid you'll be disappointed."

He walked over to where she stood in the middle of the living room, still clutching the pad as a barrier between his invitation and her insane inclination to accept it.

"Why do you think I'll be disappointed?" he asked softly. With that accented voice, every word he spoke sounded sexy and alluring. And his eyes... goodness, his eyes seemed to eat her up with their intensity.

Dahlia glanced away to break the spell he was obviously casting over her. Taking a deep but silent breath, she faced him again. "This is a business transaction, Your Highness. As I mentioned, I don't mix business and pleasure. It's not a good idea."

"I insist that you make an exception to your business and pleasure rule."

"But I won't."

"And why not?"

"Because things could get... awkward."

"I see." He stuck his hands into his pockets. "Are you saying you're not interested?"

"No, I'm not saying that."

"Then what are you saying?"

"I'm saying that it's not a good idea for me to have dinner with a client."

"I see," he said again. "Then we will move our contracts with Wane Property Management. Is that better?"

"No! That's... not what I want."

If there was ever a man to say yes to, it was this man. But because a man like Prince Kofi was no doubt used to having women throw themselves at him, Dahlia made the conscious decision not to be one of them. She certainly looked forward to the idea of dinner and conversation—in fact downright tingled at the idea. She was curious about his country and him but sensed getting involved with him could be a bad idea.

"You're only in the country for what, a few more weeks?"

"For you, I will try to stay longer." The smile on his face broadened, softening his angular features and stealing her breath. "I cannot deny my attraction to you, Dahlia, and I believe you're attracted to me too. If I'm wrong, I apologize for making you uncomfortable. That was not my intention, but I would not be the man I am if I didn't at least try. So, I am asking, humbly—which is not something I do often."

She fought the smile that threatened to overtake her lips.

"Would you have dinner with me? If you say no again, I will accept your decision, though I'll be devastated by disappointment."

She bit the corner of her lip. He knew exactly what to say. "Fine. Yes. I'd love to have dinner with you."

The resulting smile took her breath away.

"And what would your ideal meal consist of? What do you have a taste for?"

You, her dirty brain answered. "Why don't you surprise me?"

"I'd much rather take you to a restaurant where you'd like to eat."

She laughed. "Well, you'll be disappointed if I told you what I've had a taste for ever since a trip to LA last summer."

"Please, tell me."

She paused, then with dramatic flair said, "Chicken and waffles."

His eyebrows raised. "Chicken and waffles?"

She laughed at his expression. "See, I told you. I ate chicken and waffles at Roscoe's Chicken and Waffles in LA last summer when a friend and I went to visit. Sooo good, to-die-for food. Since we can't go there, I'll settle for Italian. There's a place I've been to where they make their pasta fresh and their garlic bread is to die for. Donatelli's is the name."

A charming smile lit his face. "Very well. Friday is good for you?"

Dahlia couldn't help but smile back. "Yes, and... thank you for understanding."

"Thank you for accepting."

Chapter Five

Kofi sat with his elbow on the armrest of the leather chair in his office, a temporary space set up in the hotel suite so he could work during his short stay in the United States. He spoke to his father on speaker phone.

"I haven't seen anything to suggest the buildings are falling apart," he told the king. "Except for the usual wear and tear, they're in good condition. There was also some confusion about one of the buildings that needed a new roof. Kemal was able to find the invoice and after talking to Dahlia, who talked to Melanie—her partner—there was some kind of mix-up. We're still trying to sort it out."

"Anything else?"

"Minor repairs here and there. Like I said, I believe the properties are in good condition."

His father grunted, a sound of displeasure and a signal that he wasn't satisfied with the information Kofi provided. Kofi had his own doubts. Something seemed off, but all he could think about was Dahlia's friendly eyes and anticipate running his hands down her luscious body. Immediately, his suspicions went away.

"Then you'll be back soon?" his father asked.

"I have a few more things to take care of. Personal matters."

Silence on the other end.

"You know to be discreet?" his father asked.

"Yes, I do."

"Keep me informed of your plans."

"I will."

After he hung up, Kofi gazed unseeing at the paperwork on his desk, his forefinger sliding back and forth below his lip as he thought about Dahlia and the moment she agreed to go out with him. Rarely had he ever known such unexpected joy. Never had his body burned with such need to possess a woman. It was all he could think about. Would she let him, he wondered? Or would he end up going mad with lust?

"Your Highness, may I speak to you for a moment?" Kemal stood in the open doorway.

"Of course." Kofi waved him in.

Kemal sat on one of the chairs across from the desk, his expression grave. Of course, his expression was often grave. He took his role as a member of the royal staff very seriously and was admired and respected by their countrymen for his proximity to Kofi.

"Your Highness, I have some concerns."

"What seems to be the problem?"

Kemal cleared his throat. "I have concerns about you and this woman, Dahlia. You seem to really like her."

Kofi stiffened. "What makes you say that?" he asked slowly. Although he had made his intentions clear to Dahlia earlier today, he had not said a word to Kemal.

"Your... affection for her became very clear when you decided to look at the properties with her alone, without me in attendance. You've never done anything like that before. I also know you very well, Your Highness, and I see the way you look at her. It is, shall we say, unusual." Kemal seemed to choose his words very carefully, and rightly so, because the last thing he would want to do is offend Kofi or appear as if he were trying to tell him what to do.

He made suggestions, not demands. Time for him to be reminded of his role.

Kofi stood and shoved his hands into his pockets. Kemal's face remained emotionless.

"I do not need a chaperone.."

"I understand that, Your Highness. And please, I mean no disrespect." Kemal kept his tone even yet differential. "My concerns stem from the fact that you have a certain duty to uphold, and I want to make sure you do not get distracted by this American woman."

"Do you think that I'm so weak I would forget my responsibilities?" Kofi demanded.

"No, I simply meant to remind you of—"

"Something that happened in the past," Kofi cut in, his voice harsh. "I'm well aware of the mistake I made in my youth. I was young and foolish. I'm a grown man now."

As a university student, he shared private thoughts and aspirations with a fellow student in London, a young woman he cared about and thought cared about him. Instead, she'd simply been milking him for information to sell to the tabloids. Afterward, he spent a lot of time in public service, anxious to change the narrative after the fallout. Because of such a public relations nightmare, he became diligent about his privacy and careful about his words and behavior in public.

Kemal stood and bowed his head, staring down at the carpet. "Forgive me, I have spoken out of turn."

Kofi stared at the top of his head, knowing Kemal would

not move or lift his head until Kofi clearly indicated he had forgiven him.

"I will have you know, that I intend to spend time with Miss Sommers on Friday night. I've invited her to dinner, and it would be in your best interest not to make her feel uncomfortable in any way. I am in complete control of this situation. Is that understood?" Kofi asked in an arctic tone.

"Yes, Your Highness." Kemal kept his head bent.

"Whatever I choose to do during my time here is my own decision. I am well aware of what my responsibilities are in Zamibia, and that is not something I will ever forget. When I return to Zamibia, I will fulfill my duty as required."

He hated being second-guessed. He was young but not the same foolish man he had been before. Through hard work and the passing of time, he'd shifted the populace's opinion of him. But he never forgot those years and how much he'd disappointed his family and the people of his country and had vowed never to put himself in that position again.

"Yes, Your Highness."

The rage that had shot up like tumultuous waters slowly calmed.

"I have forgiven your comments. We've worked together for a long time. I will assume they were an isolated mistake."

Kemal lifted his head, his eyes emotionless. "Thank you, Your Highness." With a slight bow, he exited the office.

After he left, Kofi resumed sitting. He released a weighted sigh and ran a tired hand over the back of his head. Dahlia could indeed tempt him from his responsibilities. There was one in particular he had to fulfill when he returned home, which was not appealing but must be done.

He was expected to marry.

He came from a proud line, a warrior line, one that had led his people for centuries.

Yes, he knew very well what he had to do when he returned to Zamibia. But after only a couple days in Dahlia's company, he did not look forward to it.

Chapter Six

Tonight was the night.

Dahlia examined her appearance in the floor length mirror attached to the inside of her closet door. She had swept her wavy hair into a top knot, loosely secured by pins.

Her outfit was simple but classy enough for Donatelli's, without making it seem like she'd tried too hard. The long, wide legs of the black crepe de chine slacks swept the floor, and the silver, spaghetti-strapped top dressed up the outfit and matched the glittery silver hoops in her ears.

She sprayed perfume on her neck and inside her elbows before slipping on a pair of low-heeled sandals. When she finished, she FaceTimed her best friend Angela.

"What do you think?" she asked.

"Wow, you look great."

"You think so?" Dahlia showed the front and back and top to bottom of her outfit.

"He's going to go crazy for you, if he hasn't already."

"Oh, stop." Dahlia placed a hand on her waist and stuck out her hip.

Angela laughed at her. "Okay Miss Hot Stuff, what's the plan? I know he's a prince and all, but you don't know much about this guy except what we looked up."

Kofi was an enigma and so was his country, because of its small size. Still, she learned valuable information during a quick search online. While there were many traditional monarchies dispersed throughout Africa in urban as well as rural communities, Zamibia was an absolute monarchy, which meant the king had unrestricted power, and anything he said was law.

Thanks to the discovery of gold mines years ago, the average Zamibian enjoyed one of the highest standards of living in the world.

"Let's see, you know who he is and what he looks like, and you already have the license plate number to his SUV," Dahlia said.

Angela confirmed all of that with a nod.

"We're going to Donatelli's for dinner. After that, I don't know. If you don't hear from me by tomorrow, call the cops. Of course, if he kidnaps me, he probably has diplomatic immunity, so nothing will happen to him."

"Don't say that!"

Dahlia grinned. "I'm just kidding," she said, though a single woman couldn't be too careful.

As Angela pointed out, Dahlia didn't *know* Kofi, but she wanted to. She longed to know what made him laugh, what made him angry, and details about his country. If she were being really honest, she wanted to get a taste of his lips and see the body beneath the suits.

The doorbell rang, and both women stared at each other.

"That's him," Dahlia breathed. Her heart fluttered in her

chest. She couldn't remember a time when she'd been this excited about a date.

She grabbed her chunky black leather purse and slung it into the crook of her arm. "Bye. I'll call you tomorrow."

"Have fun," Angela slipped in before they hung up.

With her pulse beating against her wrist like a stick to a drum, Dahlia opened the door. Kofi stood outside, casually dressed and as devastatingly handsome as when she'd seen him days before. He also smelled delicious. She wasn't familiar with the cologne, but she liked it. A lot. She also liked the black button down shirt and black pants that emphasized his lean hips and waist. The smile on his lips matched the expression in his eyes, and she damn near swooned when the smile widened as his gaze swept the length of her body in appreciation.

"Lovely," he murmured, in a low voice that sounded like he was speaking to himself.

Warmth heated her skin and Dahlia blushed. "Thank you."

"Are you ready?"

"Yes, I am."

Chapter Seven

Kofi's driver stood on the side of the SUV with the door open. As they approached the vehicle, Kofi placed a hand at the small of her back. The gentle touch soothed her nerves but ignited her skin.

He helped her into the vehicle, and she settled onto the leather seats.

"Change of plans," Kofi said, sitting beside her.

The driver started the vehicle.

"Oh?" Dahlia carefully kept the nervousness out of her voice, reminded once again that she did not know this man.

"I hope you don't mind, but instead of going to Donatelli's, we'll go back to my suite. I thought it would be better for us to have a private meal there so we can talk and be more comfortable. And I promise, you won't be tied up and stuffed into the trunk of my vehicle."

Dahlia burst out laughing. "I can't believe you said that."

"I saw your expression when I mentioned the change of plans and wanted to put your mind at ease. I have absolutely no ill intent toward you, Dahlia."

"Well, I can't deny being disappointed that I got all dressed up and no one will see me."

"I see you." He slid his hand along the back of the seat and leaned in, giving her another whiff of his enticing scent. He smelled *so good.*

Dahlia bit her bottom lip and tilted her face up to his. "What cologne are you wearing?"

"You like it?" A teasing light entered his eyes and put her even more at ease.

"I do."

"It's a special blend created for me by chemists in my country."

"Are you saying no one else can get this magnificent scent?" Dahlia asked, crossing her legs and turning in his direction.

"I'm the only one."

"Must be nice."

"It is. Care to guess what the combinations are?"

"I couldn't possibly."

"Try."

Their eyes idled on each other.

"Hmm." Dahlia bit down on the fingernail of her index finger. "I'd have to get in close to figure it out."

"Do what you must," Kofi said, a husky layer added to his voice.

Dahlia leaned closer, her nose almost touching his strong throat. She took a big whiff and then withdrew, but not as far away as she initially sat. "I don't know," she whispered.

Her attraction to this man was like no other man she'd ever met before. She was comfortable in his presence, yet off balance too. She ached to touch him and stayed close, while at the same time thinking she would be wise to keep her distance.

"Should I tell you?"

"Please."

The air around them heated.

Kofi traced a finger along the side of her face, and she felt the touch not only on the outside of her skin, but internally. As if he'd reached into some deep part of her and opened up a well of longing. They were close enough to kiss, but he didn't go in for the mouth to mouth contact, and she wasn't sure if she was disappointed or relieved he was taking his time.

"Lemon, jasmine, rosemary, Brazilian rosewood."

"The perfect combination."

They locked eyes.

"You're not like any woman I've ever met."

"I hope that's a good thing."

"It is. You're beautiful, you have a great laugh, and I can tell you have a bit of stubbornness in you, too."

She grinned. "So I've been told."

"What's your secret, Dahlia? Why are you so happy all the time?"

She'd been asked some variation of the same question before, and she had a ready answer. The same she always gave, which was sincere and from the heart. "When I was fourteen, I was involved in the accident that killed my parents. I'm alive, and I have my health. I don't have anything to be upset about. I don't worry about the past because I can't change it. Happiness is enjoying every minute I have now. I live in the moment and don't worry about anything else. Not even the future. The future will take care of itself."

His eyes clouded and his eyebrows dropped into a frown. "That's a good attitude to have. I wish... I wish things could be different."

"Different how?"

He didn't answer right away, his gaze taking on a faraway look as it flicked outside the window before returning to her features. "I won't be here for much longer."

Dahlia pulled back, watching the street lights flash across his face. Disappointment settled over her like a heavy blanket. "Well, I didn't think you'd stay here forever. I...That's too bad." The words struggled to exit her tight throat.

"I have responsibilities in my home country. There are promises that have been made that must be fulfilled."

He stared down at his hand, his brow furrowed even deeper in thought, and she wondered what the responsibilities could be. They clearly weighed him down, but she hesitated to ask, and she suspected he wouldn't tell her if she did. When he looked at her again, his eyes were no longer troubled.

"Your smile is gone because of me. I want to keep that smile on your face." Kofi took her hand in his.

"It's back," Dahlia said with a grin, though she didn't feel quite as happy as she did a few minutes ago. They had a connection, and knowing it would end in a short time sucked away some of her enthusiasm for the evening.

"You said you live in the moment. Did you mean that?" Kofi asked.

"Yes."

His charming smile returned. "Then live in the moment with me. Say you will." He pressed her palm to his lips.

"I will," Dahlia said without hesitation. Almost losing her life at the age of fourteen had taught her to appreciate each day and live it to the fullest.

He didn't release her hand. "I promise, you won't regret it. Not if I can help it."

Chapter Eight

Dahlia barely remembered the elevator ride, her thoughts stalled on the warmth of Kofi's lips pressed into her palm. She couldn't stop thinking about it, or about him. How would those lips feel on other parts of her body?

They walked down the hallway with two of Kofi's bodyguards, who'd followed behind the SUV. When Kofi introduced them, both men nodded but neither had said a word to her. One of them, Abdalla, was an intimidating mountain who stood at least six feet six with a jaw as dense as a brick. He walked ahead of them and the other guard brought up the rear.

The second man was smaller, but not small. Both exuded a lethal presence that made her feel absolutely safe. If anyone tried to attack the prince, she held no doubt they could diffuse the threat with speed and efficiency.

The guards remained outside and Dahlia and Kofi entered the hotel suite, only to be greeted by Kemal and a woman with beautiful caramel skin and a short Afro with a name tag that said Brenda. The man beside her was of diminutive size, with dirty blond hair and wearing a uniform of a white shirt and black pants. His name tag said Sam.

"Kemal, I didn't know you were still here," Kofi said.

"I am on my way out. Have a good evening." He gave a slight bow.

Dahlia, standing behind Kofi, smiled at Kemal as he passed by, but he didn't return the friendly gesture. Startled at the ugly look he shot in her direction, the smile froze on her face and unease skittered down her spine.

Why did he look at me like that? she wondered, as the door closed behind him.

"Your Highness, would you like a drink before dinner?" Sam asked.

Kofi glanced at her, raising an eyebrow in question.

"I'm fine. I'm ready to eat."

"Then that's what we'll do. Is everything ready?" Kofi asked Sam.

"Yes, Your Highness."

Kofi led the way to a wall of glass and they exited onto a balcony with a black metal railing that extended along the entire side of the building. A table for two with a white tablecloth had been dressed with silverware and plates, and chilling wine sat in a silver bucket in the middle. Kofi helped Dahlia into the chair and then seated himself across from her.

"This is nice," she commented, her gaze sweeping the nightscape.

"In the morning, I can see the sun rise from my bedroom. It's quite a sight," he said.

Sam briefly interrupted their conversation when he came onto the patio to tell them about the wine. Thereafter, he poured them each a glass and disappeared again.

"How many people do you have working with you while you're here?" Dahlia asked, taking a sip of the fruity wine.

"Probably too many by your standards, but it's quite normal for me to travel with staff and other help. I have my personal secretary, my assistant, four bodyguards, a driver, a doctor, and I also contract additional help when needed." He shrugged.

"A doctor?"

He nodded. "In case of emergency."

"What about privacy? You don't seem to have much."

"Privacy is a luxury."

"So you're never alone?"

"Rarely. In the United States, I'm not well known, but it's still important to be careful. I usually feel safer traveling in my country."

"Safer, though people recognize you as their prince?"

"Yes. The reason is, harming a member of the royal family is the only crime punishable by death."

Dahlia's eyebrows shot skyward. "Oh."

He faintly smiled. "What do you think of the wine?"

"Good choice, but I don't want to get off the subject."

"Tenacious. I like it."

"Curious." Dahlia rested her chin in her hand. "Curious about you and your culture."

"Ask me any question and I'll answer it."

"Okay. For starters, you have an older brother?"

"Not anymore," he said in a grave tone. "He and my mother passed away in a helicopter crash."

"Oh no, I'm sorry." She hadn't seen that when she Googled him.

"He was the first born, and I was the spare. Because of his passing, I will ascend the throne after my father."

"And... in your country, you can have more than one wife?" Dahlia asked tentatively.

"Correct," he replied in a neutral tone.

She had the impression he paid extra attention at that moment. Perhaps gauging her reaction to the difference in their cultures.

"Do you plan to?"

He eyed her across the table, the silence stretching between them. "I can have as many wives as I can afford. I am considering it," he replied, in an odd tone.

Dahlia cleared her throat and glanced away. She felt as if he were searching for something—looking for an answer in her eyes.

"Now tell me about you. I want to know everything," he said.

Dahlia took a deep breath, reflecting on her younger days and the sense of adventure with each trip she took with her parents.

"Well, my parents and I traveled a lot. I have dozens of albums and plenty of undeveloped film. For years it was difficult to go through them, but every so often I pick a roll and develop it."

Each time she saw her parents' faces, fresh pain enveloped her heart, but she smiled through the pain, recalling their happy moments.

"Losing my parents was tough. I was pretty young. Like I told you before, only fourteen. My... my father fell asleep at the wheel. My parents died, and I fell into a coma and was hospitalized for a while." Dahlia curled her fists in her lap.

"Dahlia," Kofi said gently, "if you don't want to talk about this, we don't have to."

She shook her head. "I don't mind. Anyway, I got banged up pretty badly, but after plenty of surgery, I'm almost as good as new." She mustered a smile.

"You are very strong," Kofi said, kindness in his dark eyes.

"Strong? Maybe. To be honest, losing my parents transformed me in a way I didn't recognize until lately. When I woke up from the coma, I emerged a new person—the way a caterpillar transforms into a butterfly. Ever since then, I've tried to live my life to the fullest." She shrugged.

"As we all should," Kofi said in a grave voice.

Chapter Nine

The server returned, this time pushing a cart before him with silver domes covering the dishes.

"I can't wait to see what your staff has prepared," Dahlia said.

With a ceremonious flourish, the server lifted the first silver dome. She gasped when she saw the food presented on the white plate.

"You didn't." She stared, open-mouthed, at the waffles and chicken on the plate.

Kofi smiled across at her. "You said you had a taste for chicken and waffles, specifically from Roscoe's restaurant. I decided to give you your heart's desire."

She laughed, the sound traveling on the night air. "I'm speechless, and that's not normal for me." She gazed across the table at him with renewed affection as the server placed the first plate in front of her. "How in the world did you manage to get this food?"

"I sent someone to get it."

Her mouth fell open. "All the way to LA?"

"Of course. That's the location you visited, yes?"

"Yes, but..." Dahlia shook her head in disbelief.

He spoke about the trip in such a nonchalant way, but the gesture overwhelmed her.

"Thank you," she said quietly.

"You're welcome," he said, also quietly. "For as long as I'm here, you can have whatever you want."

She'd never had a man say anything like that to her before.

"You're going to spoil me," she said.

"That's the idea."

The meal included sides—candied yams, macaroni and cheese, greens, and cornbread. Dahlia's mouth watered at the sight of the delicious feast and the memories the food evoked. She dug in, cutting off a piece of the well-seasoned fried chicken and dragging it through maple syrup.

Chewing slowly to savor the flavors, she watched Kofi try the different dishes, much more tentatively than she did. After a few minutes, she asked, "Well, what do you think?"

He nodded slowly. "This is good. Very good."

"All of it?" she asked hopefully. She wanted him to enjoy the meal considering he had gone to such a great effort for her.

"All of it," he said.

Satisfied, Dahlia grinned across the table at him. "I'm glad to hear that."

They ate in companionable silence for a bit. Then she interrupted the quiet with another question.

"What's it like growing up as a prince? I mean, what's it really like? I'm more familiar with European kingdoms, to be honest. Is your country's kingdom the same?"

"In what way?" He took a sip of wine.

"It seems like you would be stifled. Or maybe I'm wrong."

"There is a bit of that, but more so in my country and on the continent. Outside of Africa, most people don't know who I am. I still have to travel with my bodyguards, but no one knows who I am, and I like that. It allows me more freedom. As you pointed out, it can be very stifling to be who I am. I'm not free to travel as easily as someone like you. So, while there are definitely parks—like being able to get chicken and waffles brought to me from LA—there are drawbacks. Nevertheless, my life could be worse.

"I grew up in this life, so I don't view it as a burden in the way someone coming into this lifestyle would see the day to day duties, ceremony, and limitations. Someone new to our way of living might have problems and hate being constantly under a microscope. I've lived this way from birth. I'm accustomed to it." He shrugged, his face shifting into a thoughtful frown. "There was a time when I didn't understand the importance of my role, but I do now, and I appreciate the advantages that I have."

The last part sounded rehearsed, and the playfulness had gone out of his face.

"That sounds like something you've been told to say," Dahlia said.

"That's what I really think," Kofi said in a hard tone.

She caught a flash of something else—annoyance or what, she couldn't say. But a guard had definitely gone up around him, and she suspected she had gone too far in the questions, pried too much. She was such an open book, she expected everyone else to be the same. She needed to learn boundaries, which she had been told in the past.

I didn't mean to pry. I'm curious about you. But I've been told before that I can be rather, shall we say, nosy." She smiled to lighten the mood.

"No need to apologize. In my position, it can be hard to trust, and there are times when I can't be as honest as I would like."

"I understand."

Kofi then launched into more details about his country. The landscape, the plans for development, how they managed to be one of the few African countries that had not been colonized. Clearly, he was proud of his heritage and the efforts the country made to create an equitable society where everyone benefited from social programs, whether fisherman or executive.

She was so enthralled by his descriptions that she forgot all about her food. His rich intonation, his accented voice, all worked to distract her. When he finally stopped talking, she hungered for more details.

"It sounds beautiful, like Utopia."

He laughed softly. "My country is not perfect, but for me it's the most perfect place in the world."

"I would love to see it one day," Dahlia said.

"I would love for you to see it."

"Are you inviting me?" Her heart raced with hope.

"Yes. Would you be my guest one day?"

Her lips broadened into a happy smile. "Yes. I would love to see Zamibia."

Chapter Ten

"Chicken and waffles and now ice cream for dessert. The perfect end to the night. I am officially spoiled," Dahlia said.

For dessert, Kofi presented her with an outrageous amount of choices. Almost the same number a restaurant would offer—chocolate cake, pound cake with strawberry glaze, and a choice of ten ice cream flavors. He'd had all those options available because he didn't know her preference, and while it seemed excessive, Dahlia was beginning to understand everything was excessive in his world.

She leaned against the railing and licked away melted chocolate ice cream and strawberry ice cream that dribbled down the cone onto her fingers. Kofi had passed on the ice cream and stood beside her with his forearms on the railing, eating chocolate cake off a plate.

When they finished, the attendant came and removed the dishes. The meal was over, and a hollow sensation filled Dahlia's chest. What next? The air vibrated like a tuning fork.

If he invited her to bed, she was fairly certain she would accept, but to her surprise, he didn't.

Kofi looked at the time. "It's late. I should get you home. Thank you very much for joining me for dinner."

Dahlia blinked. She didn't know what to think. To say she was disappointed was an understatement.

"You're welcome," she said in a neutral voice.

As they moved away from the railing, Kofi took her hand and drew her closer.

He brushed a wavy curl from her forehead. "I enjoyed myself this evening. I can't remember the last time I enjoyed myself this much."

"Me, either," Dahlia admitted.

"You're confused."

She laughed shakily. "A little."

"Believe me, I don't want you to leave. I want you to stay, so I can take my time making love to you," he said huskily, his eyes glittering down at her. "But tomorrow I must leave town early on important business, and I don't want to sleep with you and then have to rush you out in the morning. Then you will regret our night together. So I will be a gentleman, though I feel very much like a barbarian, and I will take you home. But the next time I see you, I will not be so polite."

Her heart bumped against her chest the way a rubber ball would against a wall. He had no idea how turned on she was by the promise in his voice and his eyes. He clearly indicated she had a night of hot lovemaking to look forward to.

"I should have postponed our date for when I had more time, but I was desperate to see you," he added, running a hand down her arm.

If he didn't kiss her soon, she'd scream.

"Kofi." She swayed toward him.

"Yes, Dahlia." A lusty fire brightened his eyes.

"Kiss me."

His mouth twitched up to the right. Then he buried his fingers in her hair and pressed his mouth to hers. There was no tenderness in the kiss. It was passionate but not harsh. Hunger inducing. He anchored her to him with one arm around his waist while his fingers remained locked in her hair. God help her, she was close to begging him to screw her and forget whatever silly politeness he thought she needed.

His hand slid over the curve of her hip, edging tantalizingly close to her bottom but refusing to give her the satisfaction of a full ass grab. She felt all of him, the hard muscles in his thighs, the firmness of his chest, his rigid, pulsing arousal pressed against her lower abdomen.

She had never been kissed like this. Kissed senseless. She melted into him, her knees threatening to collapse under the burning heat of his mouth even as her hand smoothed over the tight coils of his soft hair.

When he finally withdrew, she raised on her toes and lifted her puckered lips to keep their lips locked together.

He teased her lower lip with his teeth and then shook his head, regret in his expression.

"Not tonight," he said in a gravelly voice, his nostrils flaring. "But I promise, I will satisfy you another day. I will more than make up for the wait."

With that, he released a sigh and pulled her into a tight, warm hug. Dahlia sighed too, disappointed, nesting her body against the firmness of his.

Kofi took her hand and led her into the suite.

On the drive back, she rested her head on his shoulder, their fingers locked together on his thigh.

When he escorted her to the door of her apartment, she took the initiative and kissed his cheek.

"Thank you for a lovely evening," she whispered.

"The pleasure was all mine."

Chapter Eleven

"**W**hy are you so happy?" Lola asked from in front of the copier.

Dahlia, who had been filing papers in the cabinet, paused and turned to the receptionist. "What do you mean?"

"You've been humming for the past few minutes, not to mention when you arrived this morning you were extra chipper. What's going on with you?"

Dahlia laughed, shrugging. "Nothing. Happy, that's all."

Happy, giddy. She'd been that way for days, ever since dinner with Kofi on Friday. While out of town, he called every evening so they could talk. She enjoyed their conversations, debating about crime and punishment and whatever other subject they chose to tackle. She particularly enjoyed hearing how much he missed her and looked forward to seeing her again.

"Uh-huh. Well, I'd love to have some of your happy pills," Lola said.

Dahlia dropped the last paper in the file and slammed the

drawer closed. "I don't have happy pills, but if I did, I would share them with you. Have you seen Melanie this morning?"

Lola nodded, pulling the duplicates she copied from the machine. "She came in about thirty minutes ago. She's working on the presentation for the chamber of commerce in the conference room."

"Is that today?"

"Yes. I think she's a little nervous."

"I'll go talk to her."

Dahlia left and walked to the conference room. Melanie sat on the table with her back to the door, scrolling through slides projected on the pull down screen. She was so distracted, she didn't hear Dahlia enter.

Dahlia placed a hand on her shoulder, and Melanie jumped.

"Hey, you okay?" Dahlia asked.

Curly-haired, with a peaches and cream complexion, her friend and partner laughed nervously. "I am, but I'm a little worried about the chamber presentation this afternoon."

"You need me to come for moral support?"

Melanie waved aside her concern. "No, that's not necessary. We haven't had a chance to talk. How did everything go with Prince Kofi?"

Dahlia toed the carpet with her right foot. "Well."

"He was satisfied with how we're managing the properties?"

"Seems that way. Although I get the feeling he has some concerns."

Melanie frowned. "About what?"

"Some of the invoices. I'm sure it's nothing, but there were a couple of discrepancies."

"Well, that's not good," she muttered.

No, it wasn't.

"Probably something goofy that our bookkeeper did. Don't worry about it. I handle the finances, I'll fix any issues," Melanie said. "Soon as I finish this project, I'll put his mind at ease. We can't afford to lose our biggest client."

"I agree." Dahlia cleared her throat. "He and I had dinner the other night."

She thought it was important to disclose that information to her partner, particularly since it could cause problems if things with Kofi went awry.

Melanie's eyebrows drew together, and she stood and faced Dahlia. "You're dating?"

"I know what you're going to say."

"No, I don't think you know what I'm going to say. This is a really bad idea, Dahlia. He's one of our clients."

"I know. At first I turned him down, but the truth is... I'm kind of attracted to him. Okay, very attracted to him."

She laughed. Melanie didn't.

"I can't believe you did that."

Dahlia's cheeks burned with embarrassment. "It's not that big of a deal. He's going back to West Africa soon."

"That's beside the point. It's not a good idea to get involved with clients, especially one so important to our business. If the relationship doesn't last or go the way he wants, he could yank his business from us out of anger."

"It's not a relationship, and I really don't think we have anything to worry about."

"I hope you're right." Melanie sounded doubtful.

Guilt nicked Dahlia's chest. Melanie was right. She had considered the consequences when Kofi initially expressed interest in her. She knew better, knew that getting involved with him could jeopardize their business, but their mutual attraction burned with the hotness of the sun. If he hadn't needed to travel, she would have slept with him the other night.

"I don't want to jeopardize the business. You're right."

"I'm not trying to be mean, but—"

"I know you aren't, but you *are* right. I don't know what I was thinking. I better get back to my office. Do you need help with the presentation?"

"No, I'm fine," Melanie said.

"Good luck." Dahlia walked toward the door, her footsteps much heavier than when she initially entered the room.

Before she could exit, Melanie called her name and she turned.

"Thanks for understanding, Dahlia."

"Of course. You don't have anything to worry about. Our business with him will remain intact. If it falls apart, it won't be because of me."

Melanie nodded and returned her attention to the presentation.

Dahlia spent the rest of the day working on several projects, answering questions via email for the newspaper, and scheduling a videographer to produce a commercial they planned to run on weekends. Though she remained focused on work, her mind occasionally wandered to Kofi and her very difficult decision to stop seeing him.

The day was almost over when the phone rang. She picked it up and heard Kofi's voice on the other end. Her heart sank because she knew what she had to do but didn't want to do it.

"Surprise. I'm back in New York, and I want to see you tonight," he said, sounding upbeat. "I'll take you to a proper restaurant this time. Perhaps the Italian one you told me about."

Dahlia shut her eyes, tamping down the excitement at the thought of seeing him. "Um, I can't tonight. I have a million things to do." She hated lying, but avoidance seemed like the lesser of two evils.

"I'm sorry to hear that. I should have told you I was coming back, but I wanted to surprise you. How about lunch tomorrow and then dinner in the evening? I'm anxious to see you."

She moved a paperweight around on her desk. "I'm going to be busy for the rest of the week and all next week, actually. I just don't have the time right now. I'm sorry, Kofi."

In the silence that followed, Dahlia heard traffic in the background.

"You weren't so busy last week. What's going on, Dahlia?"

"What do you mean?"

"Before I left, you wanted to see me. Now that I'm back, you're avoiding me."

She opened her mouth to lie, but then couldn't do it. Her shoulders dropped. "Kofi, I don't think this is a good idea."

"What isn't a good idea?" he asked sharply.

"Us seeing each other. If the situation ends badly, you could yank your business."

"You think I would do that to you?"

"You half threatened to yank your business if I didn't go out with you," she reminded him.

"That wasn't a threat. I was trying to make you comfortable by getting rid of the reason for your reservations." He expelled a heavy breath. "I admit I'm used to getting my way, and right now your refusal to see me makes me very unhappy, but I would not pull my business because of that."

Relieved, she rested the back of her head against her leather chair. "Despite your promises, I still don't think it's a good idea. Like I said before, mixing business and pleasure it's a good combination."

"I see. Well, then, I will say goodbye to you, if that's what you want. That is what you want, correct?"

No, that wasn't what she wanted. She had wanted to spend as much time with him as possible before he returned to

66

Zamibia, and when she thought of him leaving her behind, the pain of unbearable longing pierced her heart. She'd become too attached.

"I made a mistake. It's for the best," she managed to say.

"All right. Thank you, Dahlia. Have a good night." Kofi spoke in a cool, detached voice.

When he hung up, Dahlia bit the corner of her lip to fight back the twisting pain. How could she hurt so much when they barely knew each other?

Doing the right thing didn't feel good at all.

Chapter Twelve

Lola popped her head in the door. "I'm heading out. Do you need anything?"

"Nope, I'm good. Melanie said the presentation went well."

Lola pumped her fist. "Good news for us. Maybe we'll get some new business out of it."

"I hope so."

"We're growing, growing, growing," Lola sang.

Dahlia laughed. "Get out of here. Have a good night."

"You too. Don't stay too late."

"I won't."

When Lola left, Dahlia continued working on her report, her fingers flying across the keyboard. She hadn't planned to work late, but staying at the office might keep her mind off the fact that Kofi was back in town and she couldn't see him.

Her fingers floundered on the keys, and she stopped typing.

What was wrong with her? Why couldn't she get this man off her brain?

The sound of voices down the hall made her sit up straight.

She frowned, concentrating on listening. That was Lola's voice for sure, and also a man's. Was that Kofi?

Her heart tripped over itself and she shot to her feet.

She heard feminine and masculine laughter, and then Lola appeared in the doorway again. "Look who I found outside? Prince Kofi! He wanted to speak to you about one of the buildings, so I let him in."

"I promise not to keep her too late," he said to Lola, though his eyes never left Dahlia. They bored into her.

"You two have a good evening," Lola called cheerily, disappearing from the doorway.

Left alone, Dahlia and Kofi stared at each other.

He was immaculate, casually dressy in charcoal pants and a purple long-sleeved shirt that looked amazing next to his dark skin.

She steeled herself to resist him and lifted trembling fingers to tuck her hair behind her ear. "What are you doing here?"

Seeing him again forced her to relive the night they dined at his suite and the sweet burn of his kiss.

He sauntered into the office with the casual arrogance of a man unfamiliar with the word *No.* "I realized after we hung up that you said some very interesting things. You made a mistake. It's for the best. Seeing me is not a good idea. You never said you didn't *want* to see me. You never said you weren't attracted to me."

"So what?"

"Tell me to my face that you don't want to see me."

Tightness seized her chest. She couldn't do it.

"This is ridiculous," Dahlia muttered, dropping her gaze and closing the program on her computer.

"Tell me to go away for good. Tell me our conversations were irrelevant and what's happening between us means nothing. That I'm a crazy man for craving you like I crave food and oxygen."

She shut down her computer with shaky fingers and snatched up her purse, tucking it under her arm. "I don't know who the hell you think you are. You want to stay here and have a conversation with yourself, do that. I'm leaving." She rounded the desk and stalked across the floor.

Almost to the door, he caught her arm and forced her to face him. *"Tell me!"*

"I can't!"

They were both breathing hard.

His eyebrows sank low over his eyes. "Why not?" he asked in a lower voice.

His fingers cut into her arm, but she welcomed the pain. It meant that he was touching her.

"B-because I want you." She gazed up at him, knowing her desire for him was as obvious as the nose on her face. "I want the barbarian."

With a low growl, he was on her, cupping her ass in one hand and tangling his fingers in her thick hair. She dropped her purse and matched his ardor by cupping the back of his head and mashing her lips to his. He kissed her with bruising intensity, crushing her mouth beneath his. She trembled in his arms. Excited, hot, and outrageously turned on. Her panties were wet and her core pulsed with need.

Dahlia rubbed her hard nipples against his chest for relief, but it wasn't nearly enough. Capturing his tongue, she sucked hard to make it plain what she wanted. Him, inside her. Lifting a leg to his hips, she grinded her core against the raging hard-on at the front of his pants and became dizzy at the thought of him thrusting inside her.

Kofi slid his large hand along her thigh and up her dress. His finger stroked her clit, and she trembled at the fierceness of desire that flared to life inside her. She didn't care about anything else at this point. She just wanted *him*.

She fumbled with his pants, her hands clumsy in her haste. The entire time he kissed her sensitive neck and nipped at her skin. His warm breath only inflamed her more.

When she finally pushed down his boxer briefs, she dropped her gaze to take a look. She gasped in appreciation of his length and girth and wrapped her hand around him. She wanted to drop to her knees and take him inside her mouth, but Kofi had other plans. Her back hit the wall and he yanked open her top to reveal her lace covered breasts. A button popped off and rolled across the floor.

He licked the crests of her breasts and then sucked her nipples through the bra. They tightened into hard, painful peaks as his wet mouth soaked the fabric and she lifted her chest higher so he could take her deeper into his mouth.

Kofi lifted his head. "Spread your legs," he rasped.

She did, and doing so made the pounding need more intense. Wrapping his hands around her upper thighs, Kofi lifted her against the wall, and she immediately clamped her legs around his waist.

"Now, Kofi. *Please*." She didn't recognize her own voice. So low and needy. So desperate for a proper fucking.

He tugged aside the crotch of her panties. When he shoved in, she released a short cry, her head falling back, her arms locked around his strong neck.

His huge dick stretched her feminine muscles and filled her to capacity. He went deep, and she willingly took all of him as far as he could go.

His pumping hips moved with precision, each stroke deliberate and controlled. He shifted angles. He alternated the rhythm. This man knew how to fuck. He knew exactly how to satisfy a woman.

One hand slid to the cheek of her ass. He squeezed her flesh, imparting a different sensation that added to the already blinding pleasure she was experiencing. Gasping, moaning, scraping her fingers through his hair, Dahlia rolled her hips against him and relished the ride on his rock hard dick.

As the pounding rhythm increased and the tightening in her loins dragged her closer to climax, the pitch of her cries went higher.

"Yes, yes, yes," she chanted.

He muttered something in his mother tongue. She had no idea what he said, but that guttural sound in her ear was enough to push her over the edge. Her mouth fell open and her hips accelerated their thrusting movements as she chased the climax. She pulsed around him, clawing at his shoulders, out of control with the ferocity of an orgasm unlike she'd ever experienced before.

She squeezed her eyes shut, clamping her thighs tighter around his hips, hugging him so she not even a sheet of paper could slide between them.

Kofi's hips moved faster and faster. He buried his face in her neck until his body froze, and he shuddered with a deep-seated groan of satisfaction.

Neither of them moved.

Dahlia held on, suspended above the floor. She'd lost complete control. She'd even lost one of her shoes.

Finally, Kofi lowered her to the ground and picked up his pants. After they righted their clothes, he caged her against the wall with an arm on either side of her shoulders.

"I want you to pack a bag and come back to the hotel with me for the rest of the week."

She couldn't say no. She eagerly nodded.

He kissed her hard, his tongue diving into his mouth and his fingers splayed across her back.

"Dahlia, *olufeh mi,*" he whispered huskily.

"What does that mean?" she asked.

"It's an endearment, in my tribal tongue. Let us leave now." He kissed her again.

She picked up her purse, and he took her hand as if he was afraid he'd lose her.

Melanie would probably kill her, but nestled against Kofi with his arm around her in the SUV, she didn't care.

She was living in the moment.

Chapter Thirteen

Kofi pulled his body from spooning Dahlia and she moaned.

"Where are you going? she asked sleepily.

"I have some business to take care of in Zamibia. Go back to sleep. It's early," he whispered.

"Okay. Hurry back." She buried deeper under the covers.

He loved that she was demanding of his time and wanted to stay close to him. He wanted to stay close to her too. He referred to her as his beautiful distraction.

The past few days had been magical as they got to know each other better, but he couldn't ignore his work. He had a few calls to make to Zamibia, and the time difference meant he needed to do it now.

He climbed off the bed, pulled on a dark robe, and walked through the suite to his temporary office. He flicked on the desk lamp and went to work, conducting a short meeting via teleconference with several members of The Most High Council and responding to electronic correspondence, making note of the contacts who needed actual letters or cards. He would pass those on to Kemal to complete on his behalf. He had a brief conversation with his social secretary and then two more calls with other staff.

When he finished those time sensitive tasks, he turned out the light and went into the living room. He poured himself a glass of lukewarm water to quench his parched throat and stood in front of the patio looking out at the city, pondering what to do about Dahlia.

His father had given him permission to remain in the United States for a couple of months. When he left, he'd have to leave her behind, but the thought of never seeing or touching her again was an unbearable thought. In a short time, he'd become attached and couldn't fathom letting her go.

Why should he have to let her go? Contemplating the approaching dawn outside, where the orange glow of the sun fought shadows on the skyscrapers and other buildings, Kofi sipped the water as a new thought came to him.

He could do whatever he wanted. He was the prince of Zamibia, with unimaginable wealth and power at his fingertips. If he wanted Dahlia with him, surely he could devise a way to make it so. He only had to convince her to come.

He could offer her the position of his second wife. She was a free-spirited woman, so maybe she would understand. On their first date she didn't express disgust when they discussed his ability to have more than one wife.

His first wife would be the princess and eventual queen, but this way he could have Dahlia too. Surely he could convince her that this was the way for them to stay together—the best and only way.

She cared about him. That much he knew. There was no doubt the brightness of her eyes was indicative of the affection she felt. Marriages had survived on less.

Kemal's image emerged in the reflection of the glass.

"Your Highness, may I have a word?"

Kofi turned to face his assistant, who carried an electronic tablet in his hand.

"What is it?" Kofi asked, moving toward him.

"I took a closer look at the books and conducted additional research while you've been... distracted."

Kofi's jaw hardened at the not-so-subtle comment. "What have you found?" he asked, anxious to get back to plotting how he could convince Dahlia to return with him to Zamibia.

"More discrepancies."

"Discrepancies?" He sighed. "We've already discussed this, Kemal. People make mistakes. Unless you have something concrete, you're wasting my time, and frankly, yours too."

"But, Your Highness—"

"Enough of this nonsense. I'm going back to bed. You have more important work to do. I left a list for you on the desk in my office, and later today there are other tasks I need you to complete. We'll talk more when I get up later."

He turned away, dismissing his assistant and ending the conversation.

Kemal's insistence that something was wrong didn't sit well with him.

Because you don't want to see it? a quiet voice taunted.

He stopped outside the bedroom door. No. Dahlia brightened his days and set his nights on fire. He saw nothing to indicate there was a dishonest bone in her body.

Kofi entered the room and tossed aside the robe. Sliding into bed, he pulled Dahlia into his arms.

She turned to face him with a sleepy moan, and he kissed her forehead.

"Did you get all your business taken care of?" she asked.

"I did." He smoothed her thick, wavy hair and took in her features. Lush lips and a striking face. In that moment, the intensity of his feelings struck him in a new way. "You have become very important to me," he whispered.

Her eyes fluttered open. "You've become very important to me too, Kofi."

Honesty and passion nested in her eyes. He ignored the little voice in his head meant to cast doubt, meant to rob him of this happiness. No way could he give her up.

He kissed her and as always, she softened against him. He rolled on top of her, thrusting his body into hers.

For now, he indulged in the mind-numbing pleasure of the woman beneath him, away from the formality of his life and prying eyes. He intended to treasure everything—every moment in her presence, every time they made love, every conversation, and every sound of laughter from her lips—while plotting how to take her back to Zamibia.

He would do that, by any means necessary.

Thirty Minutes

Synopsis

On the way to finalize their divorce, José and Yolanda Benitez find themselves trapped in the building's elevator. By the time the doors open thirty minutes later, they have a decision to make—continue with the divorce, or start again.

Chapter One

In the back of the Lincoln town car, Yolanda placed a hand on her queasy stomach as the driver pulled in front of the fifteen-story building. She had arrived early, and soon would sign papers to terminate her ten-year marriage. The thought of starting over filled her with dread.

The driver opened the door and she slid out.

"I shouldn't be long. Forty-five minutes at the most, and that's assuming there's a problem. I'll call you when I'm ready," she told him.

"Yes, ma'am."

She walked briskly up the concrete steps to the front entrance. Her heels echoed on the tile in the cavernous foyer where visitors and employers milled about, but she wasn't ready to go upstairs yet and made a beeline for the women's restroom. Fortunately, it was empty, which gave her a moment to collect herself.

She studied her face in the mirror—sepia-toned skin and black hair freshly washed and styled into bouncy curls. The cream pantsuit fit the curves of her body, giving her a professional and put-together but approachable appearance. At least that's what she hoped her image conveyed. Inside, she was falling apart because she carried a shattered heart inside her chest.

At least she and José didn't have any little ones, both having been previously married when they met, with two children each. Neither had wanted more kids, so the dissolution of their marriage didn't include the messiness of custody and visitation because their four were all adults—three working and one in college. Splitting up the assets took the longest time to negotiate, which they completed a week ago. All they had to do was sign the paperwork.

At almost fifty years old, she would soon be single again. The man she thought she would grow old with would be moving on, and so should she.

Breathe.

Yolanda straightened her jacket, exited the bathroom, and went to the elevator.

The doors opened and she moved aside and let the occupants out. She then entered and pressed ten on the panel. As the doors were closing, a man's voice yelled, "Wait!"

She hit the button to keep the elevator open but drew a sharp breath when she saw José rush to the doors. The last time she saw him was at her eldest daughter's engagement party, months ago.

His eyes widened, and for a split second a man who spent his days making deals with no-nonsense decisiveness for his brand of tequilas, actually hesitated. Then he stepped through the doors.

"Yolanda," he said with a head nod, his accented voice a low rumble.

"Hello, José." She stared straight ahead at the reflective gold wall.

Unbelievable. Of all the people to run into. She arrived early to avoid this very thing from happening, but Fate had a vicious sense of humor.

The doors closed, and Yolanda did her best to ignore her husband's presence. Which was, of course, impossible. One couldn't simply *ignore* José Benitez. Like the tequila he manufactured, he was strong and flavorful and made other men seem more like watered down apple juice.

He had a sexy, throaty laugh and a way of looking at her that made her believe she was the most beautiful woman in the world. And his touch... *goodness.* She swallowed as she remembered how he could make her come undone. How she, a mature woman who'd had several lovers before they met, had felt like a novice in his arms as he pulled passionate cries from her throat and turned her into an adventurous, greedy nympho.

Solidly built, José stood almost six inches above her and wore one of his black Brioni suits, the bespoke jacket hugging his muscular frame and complemented by a striped tie and a blue shirt that matched his eyes. He maintained his fit body under the advice of an exercise coach. Her friends had always teasingly called her a health nut, but being married to him forced her to pay attention to her health in a way she hadn't before, and they bonded over their mutual desire to stay in peak physical condition.

They used to exercise together, five days a week in their home gym, and on weekends went running in the park near their house or hiking. Under the guidance of a nutritionist, they cooked together, experimenting with recipes to find healthier versions and complex flavors that worked together. She'd been deprived of those moments for the last six months as they hashed out their divorce, and after today, those days would be gone forever.

Pain lanced through her, and she briefly closed her eyes. She could get through this.

Neither spoke as the increasing red numbers signaled their ascent. Six... seven... eight...

The elevator stopped with a sudden jolt, rocking Yolanda into the side of the cabin. She gasped and braced a hand against the wall to keep from falling.

She looked at José, who gripped the handrail at the back.

His dark eyebrows drew together. "Are you okay?" he asked.

Yolanda nodded and straightened. "What in the world happened?"

"I don't know, but there's obviously something wrong." With an up tilt of his chin, José signaled to the blinking number eight on the screen in the wall.

He came over to her side, and the scent of his spicy cologne filled the air between them. Yolanda retreated as far as she could into the corner of the small space as he pressed the open-doors button.

Nothing happened.

"We can't be stuck," Yolanda said.

"Looks like we are," he said calmly.

"What should we do?" Her eyes searched the space in vain for an answer.

"We should call for help." José opened the panel and pressed the call button.

After a few rings, a female voice came through the speaker. "Hello, operator, may I help you?"

"Yes, my... wife and I are stuck in the elevator in the Carmichael Building."

Yolanda cringed when he hesitated.

"Which elevator are you in, sir? The number should be inside the door of the panel you opened."

José checked the number. "Elevator nine."

He spoke in a calm, measured voice, but Yolanda was starting to envision what could go wrong as they remained suspended in this box.

"Thank you. Let's do one thing before I call for help. Could you try the open-doors button on the wall, please?"

"We've already tried that," José said.

"Would you try again?"

His jaw tightened in annoyance, but he did as she asked. "Done. The doors did not open."

"Which floor are you on, sir?"

"I believe we're on eight."

"The number eight is flashing on the screen in the wall," Yolanda added.

"Can you see a light through the crack in the doors?" the operator asked.

They both checked.

"No light," José answered.

"Okay, so you're in between floors. If you had seen a light, that would mean you were on one of the floors, possibly eight as you mentioned. Here's what I want you and your wife to do. Stay calm and relax. I'm going to call for help and the fire department should be there in about thirty minutes, okay?"

"Yes," José said.

"Thank you," Yolanda added.

"Don't hesitate to call again if you need to."

The line went dead, and Yolanda locked eyes with José. "Do you think there's any chance this thing would crash to the ground floor?" There's no way he could know that. She felt silly for asking but nonetheless needed reassurance.

"I doubt it. At any rate, we should be out of here in about thirty minutes." He returned to his side of the lift and rubbed the back of his neck, a sure sign of agitation.

She felt the same way. There was no good time to be trapped in an elevator, but today of all days was particularly exasperating.

Several minutes of tense silence passed.

"We should probably call our attorneys," Yolanda said.

He glanced at her, staring for so long she thought she'd said something wrong. The problem with José was that if he didn't want you to know what he was thinking, he did a very good job hiding his emotions and thoughts—like right now.

"I guess so," he said.

They pulled out their phones and called their own counsel to let them know they were stuck and reassured them help was on the way. José finished first, then Yolanda completed her call.

"At least thirty minutes isn't long to wait," Yolanda said, to fill the silence.

"If it was too long, we both know you have no problem complaining to make your displeasure known."

Yolanda's back went ramrod straight, and her cheeks flushed with heat. "That was uncalled for."

Chapter Two

A taut, humorless smile lined José's lips. "Ignore what I said. I don't want to argue."

He looked away from her and down at his phone. He hadn't seen her in months, and the sight of her had taken him by surprise. He didn't know how to act.

It was unnerving the hold she had on him. All he wanted to do was drag her back to their home and back to their bed. He missed her. He ached for her. But this woman he had loved—still loved—had turned into a stranger. A person he no longer knew how to communicate with.

"You absolutely wanted to argue, or you wouldn't have said that."

He ignored her, pretending to scroll through messages on his phone.

From the corner of his eye, he saw her arms cross below her breasts.

"I'm not the only one who changed," Yolanda said.

He looked up then, annoyed by the accusation. "I suppose you're talking about me?"

"You used to listen."

"I do listen."

"No, you don't," she insisted.

"How can you say that? I listened to you complain about needing something to do. You started a business and abandoned it. Then there were the renovations to the lake house. You were frustrated. The designer was frustrated. I finally had to step in to complete a project I never wanted to start in the first place. Nothing was enough."

That's what hurt the most when she asked for the divorce. He had tried to fill the obvious void that plagued her, but nothing worked. Nothing made her happy. Certainly not him, and that was the problem. She no longer wanted to be married to *him*. Not only a blow to his pride, but a blow to his heart.

"I didn't want those things, specifically," Yolanda said.

"Well, I guess I'll never know what it is exactly you wanted then, will I? Because here we are, getting a divorce. Nothing I did was good enough."

He paced to the wall. He felt caged in. Trapped like an animal at the zoo. He was going to go crazy in this small space. So close to his wife yet he couldn't touch her, and he could smell her perfume and hear her voice—the lovely voice he had become used to talking to when the days were long and the work hard. She had been his escape.

He glanced at her. She stood with her fingers laced together in front of her and her head bowed.

He wanted to shake her to understand what had happened, because he still didn't know. All she said was that she was unhappy.

"Why weren't you happy? I gave you everything a woman could want. Not only material possessions, but my time too."

She lifted her head. "Were *you* happy?"

"Of course."

"Were you really? In ten years, nothing changed for you?"

José shrugged. "Of course things changed, but I was happy."

"You're a liar. You were not happy. You were not the man I married."

"And what makes you the expert on my feelings, more knowledgeable than I am myself?" he demanded.

"Because I know who I married, and he wasn't there anymore. Not inside this body." She waved a hand from his shoes to the top of his head. "After your father died—"

"Don't go there, Yolanda," he said curtly, with a jab of his finger.

"You won't even talk about it!"

"Because there is nothing to talk about," he growled. "What do you want me to say?"

"The *truth*. That you were hurting. That losing him—"

"Why would I say any of that? He was an abusive prick. He was terrible to my mother."

"She forgave him," Yolanda reminded him.

"I didn't." Rubbing his neck, José turned away from his wife. The conversation was giving him a headache. Struck by a thought, he turned swiftly to face her again. "You left me because I wouldn't grieve my father's death?"

"Of course not. The problem was more complicated than his death. You shut down and shut everyone out. Me, the kids, your friends. I couldn't talk to you anymore. The only thing we had left in common was exercise, and you were starting to pull back on that. Where did I fit in your life if you didn't need me?"

"Of course I needed you, Yolanda. That never changed." How could she even say that?

"It did change, even if you won't admit it. You changed, and I changed. When you cut me off, I realized how much of my life depended on yours. I had been absorbed into your lifestyle."

José couldn't believe his ears. "Did you hate our life?"

"We have—*had*—a great life together. I'm not complaining about the material aspects. But somewhere along the way I lost myself and who I am. The kids are gone, and when you pulled away from me, I realized I had nothing else going on. I felt all alone, and I didn't know what to do with myself. I tried to tell you, but I didn't do a very good job of it. I used to paint. I haven't painted in over eight years. I used to volunteer at the local Humane Society and play with the puppies and take the dogs for walks. Now the only volunteer work I do is write a check for a ten thousand dollar plate at a charitable event or fundraiser."

"I had no idea you felt that way. I saw your transformation is a good thing. We were growing together."

She took a deep breath and sighed as if she couldn't believe that he still didn't get it. "I was growing into you, and I didn't see it until our bond was severed. I didn't know who I was anymore apart from being José Benitez's wife. Your withdrawal forced me to take a long hard look at my life and my behavior."

"Why didn't you tell me any of this?" he asked.

"I tried, but you either ignored me or we ended up in a ridiculous circular argument that didn't have anything to do with what I needed. You were so busy hiding from the truth of your feelings about your father, you became impatient with any conversation that involved us addressing how our marriage was deteriorating. I'm as much to blame as you. I didn't do a very good job of articulating my feelings, but you—you wouldn't listen, José."

Deep sadness overwhelmed him. They should never have gotten to this point, to where divorce became the only option.

"I should have listened," José said with a heavy heart.

"You're right, I didn't want to hear what you had to say because I was too busy fighting the regret I felt after my father died." It took a lot for him to admit his failing.

They were both quiet for a few moments.

"What did you regret?" Yolanda asked gently.

José experienced the conflicting emotions that always came whenever he thought about his complex relationship with his deceased father. He moved from one end of the elevator to the other again, his right hand shoved into his pants pocket. He was suffocating in this small space. He needed to move around, but there wasn't much room to do that.

Finally, he stood still. "I never told him how much his behavior hurt me and my siblings." The words weighed heavy on his tongue, but saying them eased the tension in his body. "I... I never told him that I hated him for the physical and emotional abuse he put my mother through, or that I promised myself I would never belittle anyone the way he did her. I would never lay my hands on a woman the way he did her. I never told him that I wished she had never stayed with him for us, or how guilty I felt when I found out that's what she had done. I hated him for years, and... I never told him about the shame I felt because I also loved him." He paused. Telling his secrets left him drained and vulnerable, as if he'd been cut up with a dull knife and left for dead. For the first time he admitted out loud the thoughts that had plagued him. "What kind of man does that make me?" he asked in a hoarse voice.

Compassion filled Yolanda's eyes. "Human."

She came to him and placed a comforting hand on his biceps. As always, her touch soothed him, and he wished he could pull her into his arms and draw the strength he needed. He should have done that months ago instead of hiding in shame like a wounded animal.

"He was your father, and despite everything that happened

with your mother, he was good to you and your siblings. That's why you were conflicted. He was two different people."

"She didn't deserve that. I never understood why he treated her so badly."

"His behavior had nothing to do with her. That was all him. If he had married someone else, his behavior more than likely would've been the same."

Chapter Three

Yolanda removed her hand from her husband's arm and stepped back. He was still her husband and her instinctive response to his pain was to provide comfort.

Her husband. She needed to stop thinking of him that way.

She lowered her gaze to the floor.

"Why didn't we talk like this before?" José asked in a strangled voice, his accent thicker.

"I don't know," Yolanda said, though she suspected she knew the answer. Like a procrastinator rushing to complete an assignment, the pending divorce and being trapped in this small space forced a last minute tough conversation.

"I once heard a quote that said, '*A relationship without communication is just two people.*' That is what we became, I suppose. Two people living our own lives and fighting our own battles, separately. We no longer communicated, and that kept us from working together as a unit."

Tears of regret burned Yolanda's throat, and she fought to

keep them from welling in her eyes. "I guess it's too late now," she said in a husky tone.

A beat of silence passed.

"What if it's not?" José asked in a low voice.

Yolanda lifted her head in surprise.

"What if it's not too late for us?" he continued.

Her heart raced, but she kept her expression blank. "W-what do you mean?"

He moved closer, and she gazed up into his blue eyes. The same blue eyes she had been gazing into for over ten years. It hurt to think she would only see them on rare occasions when they celebrated special events with their children.

"I'm thinking about everything we both said, and I don't think this marriage is over. What do you think?"

Yolanda swallowed. "I'm not sure what to think. For months we've been going back and forth trying to settle our affairs. There's been so much anger and hurtful words spoken. How can we possibly get past all that and pretend everything is okay, just because we're trapped in an elevator."

"I don't think it's because we are trapped in an elevator. Being here in this place at this moment, has forced us to do what we couldn't before. *Talk.* Admit our faults and face the truth that our feelings for each other are not dead. Or am I wrong about this?"

Yolanda's insides ached. She wanted to believe and accept what he said. She wanted to believe they could have another chance at happiness.

She took a tremulous breath. "I don't think you're wrong," she whispered.

To her surprise, José's shoulders sagged in relief. Clearly, he had been as worried as she was.

He lifted a hand to her jaw. "I miss you."

He smiled, and she took her cue from him to say the words

she always did whenever he stated that he missed her. Whenever he traveled for business, it was their "thing."

"I miss you more," Yolanda said.

He lifted her palm to his lips. The soft kiss melted her heart and shoved aside her last reservations. Within seconds his mouth pressed against hers, and she opened for him.

A soft moan of intense longing drifted past her lips as their breaths mingled together. José pushed her back against the wood paneled wall, his hands gripping her hips and hauling her lower body to his. Nothing else mattered in that moment except his lips against hers and his engorged length flush against her lower abdomen, a reminder of the hot passion that existed between them before their marriage crumbled. Her knees buckled, and he anchored her to his hard body with his hands on her hips.

One hand slid to her nape to deepen the kiss. Head spinning, she embraced his torso and pressed her tongue between his lips. The taste of him was divine. Other worldly. She wanted more and ached for him to take her against the wall and quell the burning desire that roared through her body after months of deprivation. Her fingers climbed into his glossy black hair and he groaned, still weak to her touch.

His hand crept up the side of her waist and she arched toward him. Ready. Needing his touch—his hand cupping her breast, his thumb rubbing her nipple.

"Are you okay in there?"

External pounding jolted them apart, but José didn't step back. He took a shaky breath and then answered. "Yes, we're okay."

"We're going to get you out of there in a minute. We have to cut the power first. Shouldn't go dark inside the elevator, but you'll notice the lights on the number panel go out. Then we'll manually lower you."

"All right." José stepped back.

Yolanda touched the tip of her fingers to her plump lips. "What was that?"

"The promise of more to come," he replied in a velvet undertone, looking as if he wanted to eat her alive.

He bent his head and kissed the corner of her mouth as if he couldn't resist.

"How I've missed you, *mi amor. Dios.*" He spoke as if the words were torn from him, and the longing in his eyes made her ache to get out of there and go somewhere private so she could show him how much she still loved him.

Yolanda slipped her arms around his waist and lifted her nose to his throat, inhaling his spicy scent and reveling in the sensation of his firm body pressed against hers.

"I missed you too. I don't want to do this, José." Her voice wobbled with emotion.

He tilted up her chin with his finger. "Then let's not do this."

"We're going to manually lower the elevator now," a voice outside said.

With a jolt, the cabin slowly lowered until it came to a stop.

"Gonna get you out of there in a sec," the same voice called to them.

Yolanda and José pulled apart. She finger combed his hair, which had become rumpled after she ran her fingers through it. Then he took her hand, gazing at her as if his world began and ended with her. She had missed that look.

Her stomach fluttered like a barrage of hummingbird wings, and she leaned into him, content and excited for the first time in way too long.

When the doors opened, she breathed easier and smiled at the three firefighters outside. "Thank you so much," she said.

José also expressed his gratitude and they shook hands with

their rescuers. After a short conversation, they took the stairs to the tenth floor and walked down the hall to Yolanda's attorney's office. When they entered, the receptionist greeted them with a sympathetic smile.

"I heard you were stuck in the elevator." She had the thickest Southern accent Yolanda had ever heard. "I'm so sorry you had to go through that. Are you both okay?"

Yolanda nodded. "The time passed quickly, and we were fine. It was mostly an inconvenience."

"The attorneys are in the conference room. Follow me."

As they entered the room, both men came to their feet. They politely inquired about the couple's safety, and José and Yolanda assured them they were fine and uninjured while trapped.

"Well, are we ready to proceed, then?" Yolanda's attorney turned his attention to her.

She looked at José, signaling she wanted him to take the lead.

"There has been a change of plans," he said.

His attorney lifted an eyebrow. "There has?"

"Yes." José took her hand in his. "We want to put off the divorce."

"Until when?"

"Indefinitely. For good."

Yolanda smiled. "We've decided to give our marriage another try."

José's attorney appeared distraught. A frown took over his face. "Are you sure about this? Maybe you need a little time to reconsider—"

"We're sure." José cut him off with a terse tone and a look of annoyance. "We talked, and this is no longer what we want. Have a good evening, gentlemen."

José turned away and led Yolanda out the door.

As an extra precaution, they took the stairs all the way to the first floor. When they exited the building, he called his driver. She called hers and told him she wouldn't need his services for the rest of the day.

Yolanda's heart raced as she climbed into José's chauffeur-driven sedan.

"Where to, sir?" his driver asked. He didn't bat an eye at the sight of Yolanda, as if the two of them hadn't been separated for months.

José put an arm around her, and she snuggled into his body, closing her eyes in contentment.

"Home," José answered.

Happily Ever After in Hopevale

Acknowledgments

A special *Thank You* to all the Diamond Divas in the Readers Lounge! It was a pleasure chatting with you each week when a new episode of this story was revealed. Thanks for all the positive feedback. This one is for you.

Synopsis

Hunter Miller and Sable Devereaux settle in Hopevale, Georgia and discover that one of their neighbors needs their help. Soon they're caught in a life and death situation that threatens their happily ever after.

(*Happily Ever After in Hopevale* can stand on its own, but you'll have a better reading experience if you first read the story of how Hunter and Sable met in Paris, in *Almost Perfect.*)

Chapter One

The taxi pulled up in front of the house, and Hunter experienced an overwhelming sense of relief. He paid the driver and exited the vehicle with a large duffel bag in tow.

Three weeks away had seemed like forever, and he was glad to be home as usual, but especially on this occasion because of the woman who waited inside. He walked up the short driveway toward the pale blue house with white trim. The house they decided on together when Sable moved from Tennessee to be with him.

The small subdivision contained other similar homes, including a ranch occupied by his coworker, Mouse. She had been the one to suggest the quaint little neighborhood when she saw the *For Sale* sign and suggested they check it out.

The door burst open and Sable ran down the steps of the front porch. Her slicked back ponytail swung from side to side.

A wide grin spreading on his face, Hunter dropped his duffel bag as she leaped into his arms.

"You're home," she breathed, arms wrapped around his neck and legs wrapped around his waist.

He squeezed her just as tightly, a sense of relief flooding through him. He hadn't slept in twenty-four hours, wrapping up his assignment and filling out the paperwork as quickly as he could so he could get back to her.

"Somebody missed me," he teased with a chuckle.

"Me. I missed you." She ran a hand over his brown curls and gazed into his eyes.

Then she kissed him, slowly, softly.

His grip on her bottom tightened, and he groaned.

She dropped to her feet. "Come on, I have so much to show you."

Hunter picked up his duffel bag and took her hand. "What have you been up to?"

"Getting the house ready while you've been gone."

They had barely moved in before he was called away to work as security for a high-ranking government official in Hawaii. The timing couldn't have been worse. They hadn't even gotten all of Sable's belongings from out of state yet. Everything in the house had belonged to him except for her clothes and a few other personal effects.

They had only managed to paint the den when he received the call and had to leave within forty-eight hours. She had been a good sport about the interruption, but he had felt terrible.

Upon entering the house, Hunter's mouth fell open at the transformation in the living room. Sable had painted the walls, covering the ugly green with heather gray, a brighter more inviting color that served as the perfect backdrop for the linen-hued furniture they picked out before he left. The sofa, loveseat, and armchair were anchored by a tufted top cocktail table on top of an area rug.

Other touches included a bouquet of flowers on the table

and images of Paris—where they had met and fallen for each other—framed and displayed on the built-in bookcase behind the sofa.

"You did all this?" he asked in amazement.

A smile of satisfaction touched her face as she watched his reaction.

"I had help. Cruz hung the drapes and mirror for me," Sable replied, referring to the mirror between the two windows looking onto the neighbor's property. "He, Raheem, and Mouse helped me paint the kitchen, this room, and the hallways. The guys also rearranged the furniture after the store dropped off the pieces because once the movers left, *of course* I changed my mind about the arrangement." She laughed to herself.

"And you bought the chandelier," he remarked.

A plain light fixture had been in its place when he left.

"I know it was kind of expensive, but it's unique and different. I hope you don't mind."

"I don't mind at all. It looks great in the room."

"So... you like everything?"

He grinned. "You did an amazing job. Is that what you want to hear?"

"Yes. Kinda." She grinned back, lighting up her hazel eyes.

Hunter sauntered over and nudged her into his arms by gently pulling on her wrists. "You did a fantastic job, Ms. Devereaux."

"Why thank you. I wanted to complete a few projects while you were gone, so you'd come back to a nicer place."

He glanced around. "What's left to do?"

"Upstairs, and the half-bath down here. If we work hard, we can finish over the next few weekends, I guess."

"Actually, I have good news. I convinced Cruz to give me a two-week break so I can finish getting settled without interruption. And, I'll be able to help you open the shop."

Her eyes widened. "Oh, that's perfect. The grand opening is coming up and I've been a nervous wreck."

"And still you did all this?"

"I wanted you to have something nice to come home to," she said softly.

"I already had something nice to come home to," Hunter said, lowering his voice.

"Talking like that might get you laid, mister." Sable rubbed her hands up and down his biceps.

His skin rippled and tingled under her touch.

"*But*," she added, "I'm sure you're hungry. Did you have anything to eat?"

"I ate on the plane, but you know me."

"Yes, I do. That's why I cooked a quick meal. Just pasta primavera and garlic twists."

His stomach leaped and grumbled at the sound of the tempting food. "I'm ready."

They went into the bright kitchen. While she prepared a heaping plate of pasta for him and a smaller serving for herself, Hunter poured glasses of freshly made lemonade.

"This looks good." He drank half the glass and then poured himself another.

They sat in the dining alcove, and he tucked into the delicious food, eating chunks of fresh squash and peas, while his tongue danced with appreciation at the taste of lemon and the creamy, garlicky sauce made with Parmesan cheese.

He wolfed down half the meal before he finally slowed and grunted. "Delicious."

"I see," Sable said with amusement.

They ended dinner with a tasty tiramisu she purchased from Aunt Bessie's Sweets N Things, a popular bakery in Hopevale.

While Sable cleaned up the kitchen, Hunter took his bag

upstairs and hopped in the shower. They eventually wanted new bedroom furniture, but for now used what he'd brought from his old place—a king-size bed, a dresser, a nightstand, and a giant wardrobe filled with items he needed in his line of work, such as wigs and prosthetics.

He exited the bathroom in maroon boxer briefs. With the warm shower and a full belly, he felt completely relaxed. Sable was already under the covers in the middle of the bed, wearing a nightshirt and sexy as hell with her hair loose and hanging over one shoulder.

"Hey you. Missed you," she said.

He climbed in the bed and pulled her into his arms. Her soft body nestled against his, and he let out a deep-chested sigh. "Missed you too."

Now that Sable was in Hopevale, his long-term plans were finally formulating. He didn't only want them to live together. He wanted their union to be more permanent. He was ready for marriage, something he hadn't seriously considered before she came into his life.

As she flung one shapely leg over his, he tapped the base of the lamp beside the bed and the light went out.

He kissed the top of her head, and she hummed her pleasure.

"Good night, babe," he said, gently rubbing her back.

"Good night," she whispered.

Before long, they both fell fast asleep.

Chapter Two

S able sipped coffee in her home office, checking the status of inventory deliveries to the shop. She couldn't believe she was actually going to open her own antique store. Her decision to move from Tennessee hadn't been easy, but her love for Hunter felt normal and natural. The only decision was to move here and be with him.

Talking to her daughter had confirmed her decision to be the right one. Avril encouraged her to take a leap of faith and join him in Georgia. So here she was, currently a resident of Hopevale, with new friends and neighbors.

At the sound of movement, she glanced over her shoulder. Hunter strolled into the room in gray joggers and a burgundy T-shirt stretched across his chest, The Cordoba Agency logo on the front. He dropped a kiss on her head.

"How's it going?" he asked.

"Deliveries are on their way. They should be here by the end of the week."

"Which means we'll be busy unpacking and setting up, right?"

Swiveling in the chair, she turned to face him. She gazed up into his handsome face—firm jaw, gray eyes, and sensual lips she missed when he was on assignment.

"Definitely. As for today, we need to tackle the half-bath and the bedrooms upstairs."

"Sounds like a plan. Is there any more coffee left?"

"Yes, but I haven't made breakfast yet." She started rising from the chair, but he pressed his hands to her shoulders.

"I'll make breakfast. You finish up in here."

She grinned. How did she get so lucky to find a man like Hunter?

"Thank you."

He dropped a kiss to her lips, and when he tried to withdraw, she held his face in her hands and deepened the lip lock, slipping her tongue into his mouth and moaning softly when he returned the favor.

Finally they withdrew, and when he reached for the button on her shirt, she giggled and swiveled away from him.

"Breakfast, remember?" She cast a glance over her shoulder.

"Tease." Hunter braced his hands on the armrests and kissed her neck. Her skin and loins tingled with arousal. "I was tired last night, but tonight, you're in trouble," he growled in her ear.

"Maybe you're the one in trouble," she said.

He chuckled. "We'll see."

He left the room, and she sighed, feeling lucky and happy.

Thirty minutes later, they ate breakfast in the sunroom and then started to work on painting the other rooms. They quickly covered the wall in the half-bath in sage-green, then went upstairs to the guest bedrooms—both of which would be painted a neutral cream color.

They were almost done with one room when the doorbell rang.

"You expecting anyone?" Hunter asked, setting down the rolling brush.

"No. I don't think I have any deliveries today." They had ordered so many items for the house, she couldn't be sure.

"Be right back."

Hunter went downstairs, and she heard voices. Seconds later, he was back upstairs. "It's Retta. She brought back a dish she borrowed. She wants to talk to you."

Retta was one of their neighbors and a new friend. She and her husband Clyde lived across the street, and they came over immediately to say hello when she and Hunter moved in. The young married couple was around the same age as she and Hunter—in their early thirties—with no kids at the moment.

Sable jogged down the stairs. "Hi." She greeted her neighbor with a grin.

She and Retta were about the same size, but Retta had jet black hair and powder-pale skin. Her neighbor extended the dish to her. "I wanted to bring this back. Thank you so much."

"You're welcome. Anytime." She took the dish.

"You painted and did a little decorating." Retta looked around the room.

Sable nodded. "Kept me busy while Hunter was gone. What do you think?"

"I love it. You did an amazing job. One day, I hope to get our place in the same pristine condition."

Her expression turned pained, and Sable did a quick assessment. It wasn't the first time she suspected something might be wrong with the couple, but before she never felt close enough to pry.

She felt compelled to say something this time. "Is everything okay?"

"Oh yeah, I'm fine. It's been a long day already." Retta tucked a stray lock of hair behind her ear, and when she did, Sable noticed a bruise on her right wrist.

Her heart lurched.

"What happened there?" she asked gently.

Retta looked at the bruise as if seeing it for the first time. "Oh. I... I bumped my hand on the doorknob."

Sable arched an eyebrow. "That's quite a bump."

Retta released a forced laugh, eyes lowering to the floor. "Mistakes happen. I can be so clumsy sometimes."

"Like last week, when you said you twisted your ankle and fell down the stairs?" Sable had noticed bruises on her thighs when they checked the mailbox at the same time. "Retta, if—"

Retta backed up suddenly. "I-I should go. Thanks so much for the dish." She turned quickly and rushed out of the house.

"Retta!"

The other woman didn't halt, speeding across the street and into her own home.

Sable watched from the doorway, her heart clenching with concern. Once Retta was back in her house, she quietly closed the door and went upstairs.

Hunter took one look at her face and frowned. He set down the brush and came over to her. "Something wrong?"

Sable took a deep breath and looked into his eyes. "Yes. I think our neighbor might need some help."

Chapter Three

"**T**his is not a good idea," Hunter said pointedly, watching Sable place half their pound cake on a plate.

After they finished painting, they went to the bakery right before it closed and picked up a glazed pound cake. He thought it was for them, but then she explained her plan to gather more information about the couple across the street.

Sable transferred the other half of the cake from the bakery box to a cake container and pursed her lips. "Do you have a better idea?"

"Actually, I do. Tomorrow I'll go into the agency and see what I can pull up on them."

"You can still do that, but I'm curious about what's going on. You didn't see Retta. She looked shaken, and I think we need to do an assessment right away. Maybe I can convince her to tell me what's going on."

Hunter didn't know much about the couple except that Clyde was rather abrasive, but if he was violent like Sable suspected, he didn't want her going over there alone. Domestic abusers were known to strike out at anyone helping their victims. If the guy suspected Sable was trying to help his wife, he might try to hurt her. He wanted it to be clear that she had backup.

"I want her to know she has a friend," Sable added.

He shouldn't be surprised at her insistence to help. That was one of the traits he loved about her. "Okay, let's do this."

"Thank you." She raised up on her toes and gave him a quick kiss.

In the waning evening light, they walked across the street to Retta's house. Hunter rang the doorbell, and after a few seconds, Retta came to the door.

Her eyes widened in surprise. "Hello."

Sable held out the plastic container with the cake. "We brought you a gift. Pound cake."

While they stood there, the door was pulled wider and Retta's husband appeared beside her. Burly with dark hair, he frowned at them.

"Hi! Hunter's back in town, and we thought since you two were so nice to us when we first arrived in the neighborhood, it would be fun to hang out and get to know each other better. Hope you don't mind. We brought cake."

Retta glanced at her husband and the frown disappeared from his face.

"Don't mind at all," Clyde said in his heavy, gravelly voice. "That's mighty nice of you. Come on in. We finished eating dinner a few minutes ago, so this could be our dessert with a cup of coffee."

Hunter pulled up the rear as the couple led the way deeper into the house.

They entered the dining room.

"Make coffee and get some plates, hon," Clyde said, taking a seat.

"Okay."

"I'll help you." Sable followed Retta out the room and left the two men alone.

"So, how long have you lived in this neighborhood?" Hunter asked.

"Couple of years on my own, before I got married," Clyde answered.

"What do you do for a living?"

Clyde lit a cigar and took a couple puffs before answering. "Supervisor in a warehouse."

"You like it?"

He shrugged. "Can be stressful sometimes, but the pay is good. You're in security, right? I think that's what Retta told me."

"That's right. I work for a security and investigation firm called The Cordoba Agency."

"You guys have that huge facility off the highway," Clyde said.

Hunter nodded. "That's us."

Clyde leaned across the table and dropped his voice. "You have any interesting situations?"

Hunter smiled faintly. "Most of what we do is pretty routine, boring work. Not a lot of excitement."

Clyde grunted and settled in the chair. "Too bad. I was hoping we would have some cool stories to talk about. Tell you what, if I did security, I'd use it to let off a little steam. Bash a few heads in when people started acting up." He chuckled heartily, completely ignoring the fact that Hunter didn't join him in laughter.

Bash a few heads in. Interesting.

The two women came back into the room with coffee and plates. Sable sat down beside Hunter. He tried to read her expression but didn't get much from her innocuous smile.

"You two aren't married, are you?" Clyde asked, eyes narrowed.

"Honey, don't do that, please," Retta admonished in a soft voice as she stood beside the table and sliced the cake.

"I'm just saying. Hunter, I don't know you very well, but you can't risk losing a good woman when you have her. Soon as I could, I locked down Retta. Didn't I, baby?" He casually patted her bottom.

"Yes, you did." Retta gave a brittle smile. She placed a small plate with cake in front of Hunter.

"Thank you," he said.

When she moved to cut the cake again, her hand knocked the hot mug of coffee right into Clyde's lap.

She gasped, and her husband hopped up from the chair.

"Goddammit! What the hell is the matter with you?" he yelled.

Hunter tensed.

Retta backed away, eyes wide. "I-I'm sorry." Her voice quaked. She glanced at Hunter and Sable.

Clyde heaved a heavy sigh. "Don't worry about it. I'm sorry I yelled."

Retta rushed from the room and came back with kitchen towels. She cleaned up the spilled coffee from the floor, and Clyde used one of them to sop coffee out of his pants.

"You need to change your pants?" Hunter asked.

"Nah. It ain't that bad. The worst part was having hot liquid splashed in my lap, but I'll be all right."

The knife clattered against the plate as Retta's hand shook.

"I'll take that. Have a seat." Clyde took the knife.

Retta went meekly to the chair across from Hunter and sat down. "I'm sorry, hon."

"Don't worry about it."

"I'm really sorry—"

Clyde paused in the middle of cutting and glanced at his wife. His features tightened. "I *said*, don't worry about it. It was an accident. Accidents happen."

Sable reached for Hunter's hand under the table, and he squeezed.

In the awkward silence that followed, Clyde ate two pieces of cake with gusto. The other three ate less enthusiastically.

"This is really, really good. Damn good." Clyde emphasized the compliment by nodding his head.

"I'm glad you like it," Sable said. She had barely touched her slice.

They didn't stay long after that. The men ate all their dessert, leaving only crumbs. Sable ate half of hers and Retta barely touched her cake but drank all her coffee.

"She eats like a bird," Clyde remarked, sliding his wife's plate toward him and eating what she didn't.

By then, Hunter had seen enough. Right after, he made an excuse for them to leave, and the couple walked them to the door.

"Thanks for coming by. Don't be a stranger," Clyde said.

"Thank you," Retta said in her quiet voice.

Sable and Hunter waved goodbye and walked across the dark street illuminated by a few street lamps.

Once they were inside their own home, Sable swung on him.

"Did you see how he flipped on her?" She shook her head and marched toward the kitchen.

"What did you say to her when you were alone together?" Hunter asked.

Sable put the cake carrier on the counter. "I told her if she needed help, we could help her, but she refused to admit anything was wrong. I know that's typical because of her own misplaced sense of shame. And of course, she probably still loves the bastard, so she doesn't want to get him into any trouble."

"Typical for domestic abuse victims," Hunter said slowly.

She nodded, but he could tell she wanted to do more by the frown between her eyes.

"I'll find out what I can tomorrow," he promised.

She smiled, looking relieved. "Thank you."

They watched a movie on one of the streaming apps before going upstairs to their bedroom to get ready for bed.

Dressed in pajama bottoms, Hunter sauntered into the bathroom. Sable had pinned back her hair and was wearing a cute little white nightie with thin straps that landed mid-thigh. She was massaging cleanser into her skin, and a line of worry marred her forehead.

"Stop worrying about Retta," he chided. "We can't do anything tonight."

"I know. Can't help it."

She bent over to wash the foamy cleanser off her face, and he let his eyes drop to her pert bottom. His loins stirred at her tempting position.

Sable patted her skin dry with a white washcloth.

Hunter locked eyes with her in the large mirror over the sinks. "What did you think about what Clyde said tonight—you know, about getting married?"

She dipped her gaze and gave a one shoulder shrug. "Everybody doesn't need that."

"By *that*, you mean marriage?"

"Yes." She hung the wash cloth on the rack beside the sink.

"Do *you* need that?"

They should have had this talk before, but he'd been worried about rushing and scaring her off. While away he'd thought often about asking her to marry him, more certain than ever she was the right woman for him.

"I'm fine. I mean, it's nice, but it's not required or anything."

The breathy hesitation in her voice suggested she was lying, trying hard to sound nonchalant. The realization caused a surge of excitement in his blood.

"So you're cool with us living together indefinitely?"

He stepped closer behind her and let his pelvis bump her soft bottom. He braced his arm on the wall above her head. "I don't need to make an honest woman out of you?" He fought the urge to smile, knowing that phrase would irritate her.

Sable watched him in the mirror and arched an eyebrow. "For your information, that is an old-fashioned term, and—"

Three loud pops blasted outside. They sounded like firecrackers going off.

Hunter swung his head toward the sound.

"What was that?" Sable asked.

"Sounds like gunshots." Hunter flipped off the lights and went to stand at the window, peering out at the street.

Sable came to stand beside him. "Where did it come from?"

He didn't answer, body stiff with tension as his gaze swung back and forth along their street.

As they watched, Retta flew out her front door and bolted toward their house.

"Oh my goodness, that's Retta!" Sable said.

When she started banging on the door, they both rushed down the staircase.

Hunter yanked open the door, and their neighbor ran in. Blood splatter dotted her face and clothes. Her eyes were wide and filled with tears, and she was breathing hard.

"I shot him. What should I do? I think I killed him."

Chapter Four

"What happened?" Sable asked.

She and Hunter had changed out of their nightclothes into jeans and T-shirts. After placing a throw over her neighbor's slumped shoulders, she sat next to Retta on the sofa.

"Clyde and I had a big fight after you left. He accused me of embarrassing him when I spilled the coffee on his lap. I apologized, but it wasn't enough." She bowed her head and wiped away a tear that trickled down one cheek. "You were right, Sable, he has hit me before. I just didn't want to admit it."

Sable looked up at Hunter, who stood over them with a blank expression and his arms crossed over his chest.

She rubbed Retta's arm. "Then what happened?"

"I was brushing my teeth, and he came into the bathroom, yelling at me. Then... h-he hit me." She swallowed, reached up a hand to her bruised cheek, and winced. "I fought back this time because I couldn't take it anymore, but he's stronger than me. I ran into the bedroom, and he pushed me onto the bed. I scrambled across the mattress to the other side and pulled open the nightstand. He keeps a gun in there. I grabbed it, and I fired. I just... shot him. He staggered backward into the bathroom and collapsed on the floor. There was so much blood." She took a quivering breath.

"You said you're not sure if he's dead?" Hunter asked.

Retta shook her head. "After I got over my shock, I ran out of there."

"Where's the gun?"

"I dropped it in the bedroom."

"I'll go over there and see if he's alive. Call the police," he said to Sable.

Retta's eyes widened. "But they'll arrest me."

Sable squeezed her hand. "We have to call the police. Someone might have already done it after hearing the shots. Don't worry, we'll help as much as we can, but we need to get the police involved. It's the right thing to do."

Retta's shoulders slumped even further, and she nodded. "Okay."

* * *

Hunter crossed the quiet street. Several neighbors peered out their windows, but no one had come outside. He passed through Retta's ajar front door, which she'd left open when she rushed out of the house. The scent of gunpowder filled the air.

Despite knowing Clyde had been shot, he took cautious steps, ever careful. Clyde could be alive and have the gun and take a shot at Hunter if he feared for his own safety.

Hunter climbed the stairs, listening for movement on the upper floor.

The door to the master bedroom lay wide open. He walked in, the floorboards creaking under his feet. Inside, the scent of death lay heavy in the air.

He took a snapshot of the scene in his head. Blood on the carpet. A king-sized bed with rumpled sheets and two night stands on either side of it. He idly noted he couldn't tell which one Retta had taken the gun from.

He moved deeper into the room and turned toward the bathroom on the right. Clyde lay sprawled on the tile floor, the front of his shirt soaked in blood. A toothbrush lay on the floor nearby, along with toiletries that must have been swept off the counter during the altercation.

Hunter bent over the body and pressed two fingers to the side of Clyde's neck to check for a pulse, careful not to touch the body anywhere else or disrupt the blood splatter on the floor.

Nothing. He was definitely dead.

Sirens sounded in the distance, and he backed away and quickly left the house.

Outside, one of the neighbors—an older woman with rollers in her hair—approached. "Did she finally kill him?"

Hunter stared at her in shock. "What makes you ask that?"

"That man is a crude pig. One day, the window was open. I heard glass breaking and Retta yelling for him to stop. Saw her a couple of days later and asked if she was okay. She said she was, but I knew she wasn't. She wore big sunglasses that couldn't hide the bruise on her face. She denied she was being abused, but I knew she was lying." She leaned closer and dropped her voice. "I've seen it before."

"How long ago did you hear them fighting?" Hunter asked.

"About three, four weeks ago. So did she—kill him?"

"Looks like it."

The neighbor nodded, grim-faced. "I guess she finally had enough."

"I guess she did," Hunter said.

"Good for her." The woman shuffled in the direction of her own home.

When Hunter returned to the house, he told Sable and Retta that Clyde was dead.

Retta covered her face with her hands and started to sob. "What am I going to do?"

Sable slipped an arm around her. "It's going to be okay. It was self-defense."

Retta rubbed away the tears with the heel of her hands. "But the police might not believe me."

"I'll give a statement and tell them I saw you with bruises. Have you ever taken pictures of your injuries?"

Retta gulped. "Yes."

"Good. All of that is important in proving that it was self-defense."

Police cruisers pulled up outside, and their flashing lights swept across the windows.

"The police are here. We need to talk to them," Hunter said.

Officers cordoned off the house with yellow crime scene tape and handcuffed a sobbing Retta, stuffing her in the back of one of the police cars. By now, people on the block were standing outside their homes, some hovering dangerously close while holding up cameras to capture the unfolding drama.

Hunter and Sable gave statements to the detective on the scene, and so did the older woman with the rollers.

"Is it really necessary to take her into custody? Clearly this was self-defense," Sable said.

"Clear to you, but not to us. I'll be in touch if we have more questions," the detective said, walking away.

All of a sudden, a dark-haired man in a suit ducked under the police tape and made a beeline for the car where Retta sat.

"Hey! Who the hell are you? Get back!" the detective yelled.

"I'm her attorney."

"She has an attorney?" Hunter murmured.

"We called him when you went to check on Clyde," Sable explained.

A shouting match between the detective and the attorney ensued, but the attorney was finally able to speak to his client.

"Did she call anyone else?" Hunter asked.

"No, just the attorney. I got the impression she didn't have anyone else, which is pretty typical. Men like Clyde isolate their victims, cutting them off from family and friends. A place like Hopevale is perfect. She doesn't know anyone and if she needed help, she'd be afraid to trust anyone and ask for it."

Hunter couldn't argue with that logic.

Chapter Five

Hours later, the street was empty. The medical examiner came all the way from Fulton County and pronounced Clyde dead, and Retta had been whisked away to the local jail for processing.

Hands on his hips, Hunter stood in front of the window looking across at Retta and Clyde's, the house sealed off with yellow tape to preserve the crime scene.

"Are you coming to bed?" Sable asked behind him.

He turned to face her. She was under the covers, and like him had changed back into her nightclothes.

He climbed into bed but sat up against the pillows, staring across at the wall.

"What are you thinking?" Sable asked.

He glanced at her. "I'm getting a bad vibe about this whole thing with Clyde and Retta."

"What do you mean?"

"I don't know. Everything is too... neat."

"Neat? Is that why you've been so quiet?"

"Something's not right."

"You're right, something's not right. A victim is in jail, Hunter."

"Maybe."

Sable laughed. "I saw her bruises, so what are you suggesting? If Retta killed Clyde for a reason other than domestic violence, she's doing a crappy job."

"Maybe," he said again.

Sable crossed her arms and glared at him. "I'm disappointed in you. I know you've seen a lot of terrible things in your line of work, but this is exactly why women don't come forward. No one believes them. I expected you, of all people, to be willing to help. This is what you do. I, for one, will not abandon her when she needs help the most."

"I'm willing to help anyone who needs it. I'm just not sure what we're dealing with here, and until we have more info, I think you should steer clear of Retta."

"You can't be serious."

"I didn't bring you to Hopevale for you to get tangled up in someone else's bullshit."

"It's not bullshit. Right now, she needs a friend, and I'm going to be that friend."

Hunter turned on his side. "I talked to one of the neighbors, and she said there was a window open one day, and she heard them fighting—broken glass and Retta yelling at Clyde. What if he wasn't home?"

"Come on, Hunter. Really?" She stared at him, aghast.

"What did Retta wear to the mailboxes when you saw the bruises on her legs?"

"What do you mean?"

"I'm asking you what she had on. How did you happen to see the bruises?"

Sable's eyebrows knitted together in the middle. "A dress."

"You check the mailbox in the late afternoon, just about

every day, and she happened to be checking the mailbox at the same time you were? What if she was looking out the window, waiting for you to step out, so she could step out too?"

"That's crazy."

"She also just happened to expose the bruise on her wrist. For someone who has denied being abused, it's weird how both you and the neighbor have seen or heard her abuse in the past few weeks."

"Are you saying those are self-inflicted injuries?"

"I don't know. They might not be." Hunter sat up, earnest in his explanation. "Look, Clyde is definitely an asshole, but does that make him an abuser? And why did Retta want people to think or know she was being abused? Because there's no doubt she wanted people to know."

"I don't know, Hunter... I mean, you saw how Clyde acted when she spilled the coffee."

"Yeah, she spilled hot coffee on the man. He was pissed, but did that lead to abuse?"

"Did you hear what he said to her?"

"Did *you*? Think back to what he said."

Sable frowned again. "He said, 'What the hell is the matter with you?'"

"Exactly. He was surprised. The only time he became angry—or maybe annoyed—was with her constant apologies."

The light of understanding dawned in Sable's eyes. "As if he was... embarrassed."

"Right. He wanted her to stop apologizing. She was embarrassing him in front of us. And another thing, when I went over there, I took a good look at the crime scene. The bed was rumpled, there were toiletries thrown on the floor in the bathroom—all consistent with the fight she said they had. One thing was off."

"What?" Sable asked.

"Retta said she grabbed the gun from the nightstand and shot Clyde. There were two nightstands in their bedroom. From her description, I figured she must have pulled the gun from the draw farthest from the bed, except I couldn't tell which one she took the gun from. *Both of the drawers were closed.* In the heat of the moment, in a panic, you grab the gun and shoot." He transformed his hand into a fake gun and pretended to fire at the wall. "You're not going to take the time to close the drawer where you pulled the gun from. She did everything right, but that. The closed drawer didn't fit the narrative."

"It's a small detail, but holy crap, you might be right. *If* the abuse is fake, that means Retta's hiding something," Sable whispered.

Hunter nodded slowly. "Yes, but what?"

Chapter Six

Hunter parked his car in the diagonal space in front of Sable's store in downtown Hopevale, where a gold sign on the front window touted Sable's Treasures, Antiques & Collectibles. Sable turned to face him in her seat. "I want to come with you."

He shook his head. "You can't, babe. You have a delivery coming for the store."

She sighed heavily, groaning because she knew he was right.

He took her hand and squeezed. "As soon as I know something, I'll let you know."

"I guess I'll have to be patient." She blew out a frustrated breath and pouted.

Hunter leaned over and kissed her soft lips, prompting a smile to her mouth. She tasted sweet, like honey, and smelled good too.

Keeping his face close to hers, he gazed into her hazel eyes. "Shouldn't take long. I'll get Raheem to help me and then I'll come back and help you out here."

The day before, they completed painting the rooms and upstairs hallway. Today they were going to work in the store, but Hunter wanted to do some digging first.

He had already intended to look into Clyde and Retta's background, but the events two nights ago made him more determined to do so. Clyde's death was suspicious. At the Cordoba Agency, he would have Raheem, the VP of technology, research their backgrounds. If anyone could find out if something was awry, Raheem could.

"Okay. I'll talk to you later." Sable reluctantly climbed out of the vehicle.

Hunter waited until she was inside and waving to him from behind the locked door before he pulled away.

The Cordoba Agency headquarters was a huge campus off the highway. Once he drove onto the property and went through the biometric scanning procedures, Hunter made his way to Raheem's modern-looking office filled with glass furnishings and multiple monitors.

He rapped the open door's frame, and Raheem looked up from his computer.

"Hey, what's going on?" He grinned and rolled his shoulders. Brown-skinned with a hawkish narrow nose, Raheem had once been a ladies' man but gave up his wild ways for the woman he loved.

Hunter strolled in. "Too much. I know you didn't expect to see me for a couple of weeks while Sable and I settled into the house and got her store up and running, but like I told you over the phone, something's going on with my neighbor across the street. At least I think so. I could be wrong."

Raheem frowned. "What's going on?"

Hunter gave him the rundown and told him about his suspicions that all might not be what it seems with Retta, the grieving widow.

"Interesting. Let's see what we can find out."

Hunter moved to stand behind the desk and looked over Raheem's shoulder. He watched as his friend and co-worker plugged in Retta's first and last name and cross-referenced it with Clyde's. His name pulled up a full history, showing where he went to school, birthplace, where he worked, credit cards, etc. Her data was significantly scant.

Raheem slowly scrolled down the page of information. "Not much to see."

"Like someone hiding their identity."

"The only people who don't leave any type of trail are those actively trying to eliminate themselves from online. Based on the info in front of us, she came into existence only a couple of years before she married Clyde."

Hunter braced both hands on the desk. "I knew it. I knew something wasn't right."

Raheem rubbed a hand across his jawline. "You wouldn't happen to have a photo of her, would you?"

"Nah, but I could probably get one. Oh, wait a minute. She came over to the house twice this week, which means she would have been recorded on the doorbell video."

He lifted his phone from his pocket and pulled up the video from when Retta came over and he and Sable were upstairs painting. He showed it to Raheem.

"Send it to me."

After Raheem received the video, he took a still of Retta's face. "We have new facial recognition software that should be able to pick up her online presence."

Hands crossed over his chest, Hunter watched as the computer ran through the faces of women around the country.

After a dull beep, the software stopped scrolling and an image of Retta popped up on the screen with short platinum blonde hair and a different name with a California address.

"Well, well, well..." Hunter murmured.

The software continued working and then another beep. This photo showed Retta with yet another name, but with dark hair like she wore now.

"Now we know why we couldn't find any information on her," Raheem said.

Minutes later, another beep, and another image of his neighbor, this time with red hair.

Hunter cursed under his breath.

The computer continued searching but didn't lock on any other images.

"Three different names."

"Let's see who these women are," Raheem said. He tapped the keyboard several times.

They spent the next hour reviewing the information. By the end, Hunter knew way more about Retta than he ever expected to learn. Raheem sent the pages to a printer on the credenza behind him and handed them to Hunter.

Hunter shuffled the pages. "Married three times before Clyde, and all her spouses are dead."

"Ain't nobody that unlucky. What are you going to do?"

"Take this to the police. Let them handle it."

"Holler if you need me."

Working with such an excellent team in the security and investigative industry meant Hunter could trust and call on a number of people if he needed help, for which he was grateful.

"I will. Thanks."

He left the compound and drove to Sable's shop. Since it was later in the day, a few people strolled along Main Street, going in and out of the stores and other businesses.

The old bell on the door rattled, and Sable came from the back, her expression anxious as she maneuvered through the boxes and antiques on the sales floor.

"What did you find out?" she asked, resting her hands on her hips.

"You're not going to believe this." Hunter handed over the sheets of paper and watched in silence as she reviewed them.

"She's been married a total of *four* times in the past ten years?" She glanced up at him.

"Each time under a different name, and all of her previous spouses died. The old guy died in his sleep, and she received the house and everything in his bank accounts and brokerage account. His kids got nothing. The woman in California fell off the side of the mountain when they went hiking, and Retta received a million dollar payout. The man she was married to before Clyde died when his car ran into a tree on a sharp curve. He lost control of the vehicle when his brakes mysteriously failed. She received another million dollars in life insurance, plus an accidental insurance policy payout."

Sable frowned, gazing down at the documents. "The fifty-thousand dollar policy on Clyde isn't much in comparison."

"It's not, and self-defense or not, she killed him, which means she's unlikely to receive the money even though she's listed as the beneficiary. At the very least, she'll be tied up in legal paperwork for months—possibly years. But I'm certain she's not interested in that meager policy. Go to the second to last page, with the information on Clyde. Look at the paragraph near the bottom."

Sable shuffled the papers and trained her eyes on the end. She gasped. "His aunt left him a Liberty Head nickel a couple of years ago?"

"He must have mentioned it to Retta while they were dating," Hunter said. "Raheem found his safe deposit box at the local bank, which is where he probably has the coin stored. We found out it's worth millions."

"Easily. There are only five in existence, and the last one

sold for $4.5 million four years ago. Clyde lives in a modest house in a small town and works a job he hates, but he was sitting on a fortune."

"And Retta knew it."

"Hunter, we have to tell the police. We can't let her get away with this again."

"I agree. Your delivery already came?"

"Yes, the boxes are in the back. I'm ready to roll."

He grinned. He loved her can-do attitude. "Let's do this."

Chapter Seven

"What do you mean there's nothing you can do?" Hunter's voice echoed in the nondescript interrogation room as he stared across the table at Detective Frank, the officer assigned to Retta's case.

The detective shrugged, tilting back his chair in an irritatingly negligent way.

"I'm sorry. We don't have the resources to chase down false leads."

"You're the Atlanta Police Department. The very reason the case is on your desk is because of your resources."

Because of Hopevale's small police force, the Atlanta police took the lead on the investigation. They had more manpower and advanced forensics.

"We're investigating the death because of our relationship with the Hopevale police, but from what I can see, there's no foul play here. Didn't you and your wife say you saw bruises on Ms. Sharp?"

Sable stiffened when the detective said *your wife*. Her reaction reminded Hunter that when he'd asked her about marriage a couple nights ago, she'd stated it's 'not required.' She'd been a terrible liar in Paris and was a terrible liar now. If his hunch was correct, they wanted the same thing—to be bonded together in a committed, legally binding relationship.

"Retta obviously tricked us," Sable interjected. "She wanted us to see the bruises. Can't you see that?"

"All I see, is that the two of you have come up with some cockamamie story about her faking her bruises—that *you* said you saw. Hell, even the neighbor heard them fighting one day and saw bruises on the woman. And wouldn't her husband notice her bruises?"

"The bruises could have been self-inflicted to sell the story of abuse, and she could easily lie to her husband about how she got them," Sable said.

The detective arched a skeptical eyebrow.

"What about the fact that she's had three other spouses?" Sable asked.

The detective shook his head. "Doesn't prove anything except she's the kind of woman people want to marry. So maybe she falls in love fast. That's not unusual. Ms. Sharp was not involved in any of those other deaths. They were ruled accidents, or in the case of her older husband—the man died of old age."

Hunter fisted his hand on his thigh. "You don't find it strange that *all* of her spouses died, and each time she's been the beneficiary of their estate?"

"She was married to them. Of course she'd be the beneficiary."

This guy couldn't be serious.

"What about her different names?" Hunter asked.

"That's... admittedly unusual..."

"*Unusual?*" Hunter repeated in a caustic tone.

The detective shot him a dark look. "Unusual but not

139

illegal."

Sable placed a hand on Hunter's arm to calm him.

"Detective," she said in her sweetest voice, "would you at least consider looking into this further?"

He glanced at Sable and his expression softened, which made Hunter want to throttle him.

"I'll see what I can do. I'll look into it."

"Thank you," Sable said.

"I'm not making any promises," Detective Frank added quickly. "I'll call Ms. Sharp and ask her to come in for questioning, but I can't force her to."

"What do you mean, 'come in'? She's not in police custody?" Hunter asked.

The detective shook his head. "Her attorney got her released this morning. She's been told to stay close, but we really don't have any reason to hold her or limit her movement. Seems like a clear cut case of self-defense."

"What's her attorney's name?" Hunter asked.

"Why?"

"Just curious," Hunter answered.

Both men stared at each other for a brief moment. Tension crackled in the air. Hunter did his best not to appear confrontational so he could get the information he wanted.

Detective Frank opened the file. "Jeremiah Bivens. Listen, Ms. Sharp had photos of her bruises, there was evidence of a struggle, and we have reports from you two and the neighbor corroborating that she was abused. We sent everything to the D.A., but we don't foresee him pursuing charges at this point."

"But if there's a pattern of her spouses dying..." Sable said, her voice hopeful.

"Maybe a pattern, maybe not. She could just be very unlucky. Again, there was no evidence of foul play in her previous marriages. I'll do what I can, but don't get your hopes up." The detective shot a dismissive smile across the table at them.

"Thank you," Sable said, sounding defeated.

Hunter couldn't bring himself to say thanks. The guy was a lazy bum who clearly didn't want to be bothered doing one thing extra. He wanted everything tied up neatly so he could move on. Case closed.

He stood and Sable stood too.

"You're welcome," the detective said pointedly, looking at Hunter.

Ignoring him, Hunter placed a hand at the base of Sable's spine and ushered her toward the front door. Outside, he stopped on the sidewalk and gazed out at the parking lot.

"What are you thinking?" Sable asked.

He looked down at her. "You and I both know Retta murdered her spouses. She shoved her wife off the mountain, she messed with her husband's brakes, and she probably suffocated the old man. And Clyde... I'm more convinced than ever that she shot him in cold blood and is using domestic violence as an excuse."

"Which makes me sick. She's making a mockery of real victims. Meanwhile, she's nothing but a black widow!"

"Detective Frank isn't going to do shit, and if Retta was released this morning, she won't stick around in Hopevale much longer. If she hasn't already, she's going to retrieve the coin from the bank and skip town."

"Which means she'll get away with murder again. I can't believe this."

"She's not going to get away with it," Hunter said in a determined voice.

Sable's face brightened. "You have a plan."

"Hell yeah, I have a plan. If Detective Frank won't stop her, I will."

Chapter Eight

Standing in the dark of the living room, Sable peered out the window while Hunter was in Retta's house across the street. Night had fallen, and the shadows hugged the houses now the streetlights were on. He had gone through the back door under cover of darkness. She had wanted to go with him, but he insisted she stay behind and keep watch in case Retta returned while he was inside the house.

With so many homeowners having security cameras, Hunter used a Wi-Fi jamming device to temporarily block the feeds so there would be no record of him going to the house across the street.

His plan was simple. Find the key to the safe deposit box to keep Retta from taking the coin and leaving town.

When the police arrested her, she didn't have her keys. Nothing but the clothes on her back. With their doorbell camera trained across the street, they saw no evidence she had returned since the police tape went up, though she'd been released yesterday.

After Hunter got the coin, they would confront Retta, with

the intention of getting her to confess her crimes while secretly recording the conversation. It was a long shot, but Retta was essentially a serial killer—a unique group of murderers often manipulative, intelligent, and narcissistic. She would not take kindly to having her plans thwarted. Despite her meek appearance, her hubris and narcissism would be key to bringing her to justice—if they handled the situation correctly.

Sable watched a white car roll past the house and pull into a garage a couple of doors down.

"Got them. Found both sets of keys in the tray by the door." Hunter's voice came through the phone attached to her ear.

"Can you tell which one is the safe deposit key?"

"Yeah, it's on the keychain for Clyde's truck and pretty distinct. If there's another one, it's not on her keychain."

Sable breathed easier. "Get out of there before she has the same idea you do and says screw the police tape and comes to get the key."

"Yes, ma'am."

She smiled briefly at his teasingly sarcastic tone, but tension rested in her shoulders until shadowy movement on the side of Retta's house signaled Hunter was coming toward the front.

A tan SUV came cruising down the street.

"Wait!" she whispered.

Hunter stopped moving, and she held her breath.

The vehicle continued down the block and then turned down another street.

"Now," Sable said, speaking quietly though no one else could hear her.

Hunter strolled across the street, moving casually in all black. When he entered the house, Sable let out an audible sigh of relief.

Hunter flipped on the light and opened his palm to show the key.

"There it is," she said.

He nodded. "Won't be long now. First thing in the morning, I'm going to pick up the fake ID at the office. I'll be at the bank, ready to go in when it opens at nine."

Raheem had promised him a fake ID with the name Clyde Sharp, which he'd use along with the key to gain access to the bank box.

"I hope this works," Sable said.

Hunter turned off the Wi-Fi jammer. "It will. I don't anticipate anything going wrong. Then when we get the evidence, I'll shove it up Detective Frank's ass."

Sable let out a little laugh. "You really don't like that guy."

"Not one bit, and I really don't like the way he looked at you."

"He was not looking at me in any kind of way," Sable said.

Hunter grunted and started up the stairs.

Sable followed. "You think because you're attracted to me, every man is attracted to me."

"You think they aren't?" He tossed the question over his shoulder.

"It's flattering, but no, I don't think so."

In the bedroom, Hunter hauled his shirt over his head and tossed it in the hamper.

"You sure you don't want me to come with you tomorrow?" Sable asked.

"No. Anything goes wrong, I don't want you tied to this." He continued undressing, and her eyes lingered on his tight abs and muscular thighs sprinkled with dark blond hair.

Sable tilted her head at him. "You know I can handle myself."

"I know, but I'd rather you didn't have to." He sauntered over to her and kissed the tip of her nose. "Let's go to bed. I have an early morning."

He pulled her blouse over her head and tossed it on the floor. Then he started on the zipper in her jeans.

"I get the feeling you don't want to go to bed to sleep," Sable said.

He gazed up at her from his crouch on the floor, gray eyes alight with hunger as he slowly tugged down her jeans. "You know me so well. This little adventure has me riled up."

"I know how you get when you're riled up," she said huskily.

The first time they made love in Paris had been after a particularly adrenaline-filled race from pursuers. Interesting how danger made them both horny.

After he'd removed her denim pants, Hunter peeled her lace panties down her hips while she unhooked her bra. Both pieces of lingerie hit the floor at the same time.

He remained in the lowered position and skated his hands up her toned legs, tracing her hips to her lean waist. His touch dragged heat over her skin and made between her thighs ache with anticipation.

Finally, Hunter stood, cupping her bare bottom in both hands.

"I think you're a little riled up too," he said.

"I am."

Sable looped her arms around his neck and dragged his lips to hers. When they kissed, the ache in her loins tightened into a twisting pain as his hard chest pressed into her nipples. They moved onto the bed, his hair-roughened legs parting hers, and his lips devouring her like a starving man.

* * *

Sable groaned and turned away from the light pouring into the room. Burrowing deeper into the rumpled bed sheets, she pressed her nose into the pillow and inhaled the scent of cucumber-mint Hunter left behind.

She sighed. God, she loved this man. So much at times she couldn't think straight and wanted to spend every waking moment with him. She vaguely recalled him leaving earlier this morning, but she'd been half asleep. He kissed her forehead and whispered *I love you* before he left.

Last night had been magical and needed. He'd taken his time kissing every inch of skin, sucking her nipples, stroking between her legs, and in general making her feel like a goddess in his arms.

She sighed again, this time allowing a faint smile to cross her lips.

Slowly, the smile died as she thought about their future. When this mess with Retta concluded, they needed to have a heart to heart. She hadn't been completely honest with Hunter about her desire for marriage because she'd worried about chasing him away. Talking marriage seemed premature since they hadn't known each other long, but being afraid to be open and honest and reach for the prize of his love had almost made her lose him before. She wouldn't risk making the same mistake again.

He loved her. She loved him. She should be confident in their feelings for each other and their future.

"No more doubts, Sable," she chided herself aloud.

She rolled onto her back and squinted against the sunlight, shoving her tangled hair out of her face with both hands.

The phone rang, and she reached for it on the nightstand. "Hello?"

"Sable? This is Roland."

"Hey, Roland. What's up?"

Roland ran a small cafe on Main Street, and they struck up a friendship because sometimes she went there for morning coffee or a sandwich at lunch.

"There are a bunch of boxes outside your back door. I noticed them when I went to the dumpster, but didn't see your car parked out front."

Sable sat up. "What?"

"Yes, ma'am. You coming to the store today?"

"I hadn't planned to. I received a delivery yesterday and didn't expect anything else until next week. Thanks for the heads up, Roland."

"Not a problem. Us small business owners gotta look out for each other."

"I appreciate it. I'll be there in a bit."

Darn it.

So much for enjoying a lazy Saturday morning in bed while she waited for Hunter's return. Sable rolled off the mattress, planting her feet on the floor and pushing up with a groan. She glanced out the window and froze. The police tape was gone, and an unfamiliar black sedan sat in Retta's driveway. Looked like someone was in the driver's seat, but she couldn't tell for sure.

Was Retta back?

She snapped a photo of the vehicle and sent Hunter a text.

As she brushed her teeth, he responded. *I'll forward this to Raheem.*

R U almost done? she asked.

Waiting for the bank manager.

She texted back. *Everything okay?*

He's the only one who can give me access to the box. He gets here at 10.

147

That sucks. I'm going to the store. Roland told me a shipment is sitting at the back door.

K. I'll let you know when I'm done here.

Chapter Nine

Sable pulled on a T-shirt and jeans and jogged down the stairs. She climbed into her car in the garage and let the door up. Easing backward down the drive, she saw Retta come out of her house. She pretended not to see her, but the other woman raced across the street.

Sable hit the brakes. *Shit.*

She calmed down. She didn't want to tip off Retta that they knew about her black widow past.

Retta came up to the window and Sable rolled it down.

She barely recognized her neighbor. Pink lipstick added color to her lips, her pale skin glowed, and her black hair was styled in loose waves that cascaded past her shoulders. She looked much better than when Clyde was alive. Killing her husband agreed with her.

"Hi. I never thanked you for the other night. You and Hunter were so kind to me," Retta said.

"You're welcome. I guess everything worked out?"

"Well, almost." She tossed a glance at the house. "Is Hunter here?"

"No, he had an errand to run."

"Oh. Do you mind if I talk to you for a few minutes?"

Sable wrinkled her nose. "Can't. I'm on my way to my store."

"It'll just take a few minutes, I promise. I need someone to talk to about my traumatic experience, and you and Hunter are the only friends I have in Hopevale." Her lips flattened into a rueful line that begged for sympathy.

Alarm bells going off in her head, Sable gripped the steering wheel. "I'm really sorry. If I don't get to the store—"

Retta lifted the left side of her shirt and showed the pistol stuck in the waistband of her trousers. "Get out of the car, Sable."

Time stood still, but Sable's heart galloped with fear. "I... don't know what's going on, Retta. I thought we were friends. What are you doing?"

Retta's sinister smile frightened her more. "Get out of the car, and don't do something stupid like honk the horn, or I'll put a bullet in the middle of your face. Forget about driving away."

She shot a sideways glance at the street, and Sable saw the black sedan pull across the driveway, blocking her in. She immediately recognized the dark-haired man behind the wheel. Jeremiah Bivens, the attorney!

"Get out. Now," Retta said.

Sable took a calming breath and picked up her purse from the passenger seat.

"Leave the purse. I'm not an idiot."

The bag contained her phone, and she'd hoped to sneak a call to Hunter. She carefully returned it to the seat and slid out of the vehicle.

"I don't know what's going on with you," Sable lied, hoping that by feigning ignorance she could keep Retta from violence.

"I'll explain everything once we're inside."

Sable opened the front door and let them into the house.

"Kitchen," Retta said.

She moved stiffly into the kitchen, and they sat across from each other. Sable folded her hands in her lap while scanning the counters for something she could use as a weapon.

Retta stared at her. "You know, don't you?"

Sable swallowed, gut tight with apprehension. "Know what?"

The corner of Retta's mouth twisted up. "About me and my past."

"I don't know what you're talking about."

"No? My attorney received a call yesterday from Detective Frank. He wanted me to come in for questioning. Seems two of my neighbors provided him with information that cast doubt on whether or not I killed my husband in self-defense."

Detective Frank and his big mouth.

"What does that have to do with me?"

Retta's eyes narrowed. "He didn't tell me which neighbors, but I know it was you and Hunter. Where is it?"

"Where's what?"

She leaned forward. "The key."

The beat of Sable's heart ratcheted up faster.

"What key?"

Maybe by stalling, Hunter would arrive before something bad happened.

"Don't play dumb. The key to Clyde's safe deposit box is gone, and I know the police didn't take it. I need that key."

"Why?" Sable challenged her with a stare, though she and Hunter had already guessed.

"I said don't play dumb. You know about the coin. It's mine."

Sable licked her dry lips. "You don't have another key?"

"No! I can get into the box, but Clyde had the only key and kept it on his keychain. He wasn't a complete idiot," Retta spat.

"Maybe Clyde removed the key before he died. If you wanted the coin so bad, you should have taken the key off his keychain when you had the chance."

"What would be the fun in that? Better to get rid of him." Suddenly, Retta straightened, and she frowned. "Wait a minute, where is Hunter?"

The question took Sable off guard. "At work."

Retta's eyes narrowed. "You said he was running an errand."

Crap. Why was she such a bad liar? "He went to work and then had to run an errand."

"Right," Retta said, shaking her head. "I didn't think much about it when he mentioned he worked for the Cordoba Agency, but now I see that's where I messed up. I researched them, and they have all sorts of resources. Somehow he figured out how to get the coin, didn't he?"

"Why would he—"

"Tell me the truth!" Retta shoved the gun in her face. "If he didn't get the coin, then I can kill you now so you don't talk. Did he go to get the coin?"

Sable closed her eyes and then opened them. "Yes," she answered past a tight throat.

"Perfect. You're coming with me."

"Where?"

"Don't worry about that. Let's go." Retta stood.

"Are you going to kill me?" Sable rose slowly from the chair. Fear beat hard in her chest.

"Not yet. I need you alive, in exchange for the coin." Retta waved the gun toward the entrance to the kitchen, indicating Sable should precede her.

Sable moved ahead but realized this might be her best

chance for escape. She might not get another chance. With a swift turn, she knocked Retta's gun hand to the left. A shot fired into the wall. She followed up with a quick palm heel strike to the nose. Retta screamed in pain and fell backwards. The gun slipped from her hand and skated across the tile floor before crashing into the base of a cabinet.

Before Sable could retrieve the weapon, the front door was flung open and Jeremiah burst into the house. He must have been standing right outside. No way he could have made it from the car to the door that fast.

Sable leaped over Retta with the intention of escaping through the back door, but she grabbed Sable's ankle and she went crashing to the floor, landing hard on her hands and knees. She kicked off the other woman's hand and scrambled to get up, but Jeremiah pounced on her. He grabbed a handful of her thick hair, and she cried out in pain as he yanked her to her feet.

Tears sprang to her eyes as she clutched his hands to ease the pain.

"Keep still."

A powerful backhand slap landed on her cheek. Sable cried out again, flinching as the stinging blow vibrated along her skin. The metallic taste of blood filled the inside of her mouth, and she staggered, almost collapsing under the force of the strike.

Jeremiah grabbed her arms and yanked her back against him. Retta picked up the gun and glowered at her. Blood leaked from one nostril of her reddened nose, and she angrily wiped it away. "I think you broke my nose. I should shoot you."

She lifted the gun, and Sable tensed and averted her gaze.

Retta lowered the gun. "We need to get out of here, and we're taking her with us."

"Why? What about the key?" Jeremiah asked.

"I'll explain in the car. Let's go before one of the nosy neighbors calls the cops, or before Hunter returns."

Jeremiah hauled Sable toward the front door.

"Don't utter a sound, or I'll shoot you, and not to kill you," Retta said.

The three exited the house and piled into the sedan. Jeremiah drove while Retta held the gun on Sable in the back.

Sable slumped against the seat and touched her burning right cheek.

Her only consolation was knowing Hunter would never let them get away with this.

Chapter Ten

"**B**abe, I just left the store, and you weren't there. I put the boxes inside, and I'm on my way home. Where are you?"

Frowning, Hunter hung up after leaving the voice mail. He didn't want to overreact. That was easy to do when it came to Sable, but it was unusual that he hadn't heard from her.

He had worn a disguise to the bank, and after he left he removed the wig, blue eyes, and mustache and sent her a text, but she never responded. He thought she might be busy and went by the store, but she wasn't there, and Roland at the cafe said he hadn't seen her.

When he finally pulled into their neighborhood, his frown deepened at the sight of Sable's car in the driveway and the raised garage door. He parked in the street, eyes sweeping the area. Nothing caught his attention, except the police tape was gone from Retta's house. He climbed out of the car and went to Sable's vehicle.

He peered inside. Her purse was on the passenger seat. As a former thief, she would never leave her purse unattended, even in their driveway. The skin on the back of his neck prickled. Something was definitely wrong.

He bent to retrieve the knife from his ankle holster, when the older neighbor who walked around with rollers in her hair rushed toward him in a turquoise muumuu.

She clutched her chest, panting hard. "I'm so glad you're here. I didn't know if I should call the police or not."

"What happened?" Hunter asked.

"I saw Retta—the young woman from across the street—and Sable with a man I didn't recognize leaving in a black car. The whole thing was odd because Sable didn't close the garage door, and the way they moved—her and Retta—as if Retta was forcing her into the car."

Hunter's heart rate spiked with alarm. "Thank you for that information."

"You're welcome. Do you need me to do anything?"

"No, go back to your house. I'll look into this myself."

The woman nodded, though a worried frown remained on her face. She scurried back to her house, and Hunter took Sable's purse from the passenger seat. He walked to the front door and turned the knob. Unlocked. Another sign something was wrong. Sable would never leave without locking the door. He placed her purse on the living room table and remained in one spot, listening, in case someone the neighbor hadn't seen was in the house.

Convinced he was alone, he walked toward the kitchen and stopped abruptly when he saw a bullet hole in the wall. He rubbed his finger over the marred sheetrock and did a quick scan of the floor. No blood anywhere. A wild shot, maybe?

In the kitchen, he righted an overturned chair, which indicated a struggle had taken place. He bent toward a blood smear on the tile. Someone had been injured. Possibly Sable, or someone else if she put up a fight. Knowing how feisty his woman was, he didn't doubt she did.

He checked the doorbell camera's video feed and saw the moment Retta came from next door and stood beside Sable's vehicle. Although he heard their voices, he couldn't hear exactly what they said because of the distance from the camera.

He watched the attorney, Jeremiah Bivens, rush into the house and held his breath, gut taut when they all left and Retta threatened to shoot Sable if she made a sound. Then anger rose inside him when he saw Retta push Sable into the backseat of the car and they drove away.

Where could they have taken her?

As if in answer to the question, a text popped up on the screen. He read the contents and his blood ran cold.

If you want to see Sable alive again, bring the coin to the east end of Maplewood Nature Preserve at 8 p.m. No cops. No weapons. Or we kill her.

A blocked number. Hunter released a roar of anger and gripped the phone, fighting the urge to slam it into pieces on the tile.

Taking a deep breath, he read the message again to see if he'd missed anything, but he hadn't. They kidnapped Sable and wanted the coin in exchange for her safe return. If anything happened to her, he'd never forgive himself for getting her tangled up with Jeremiah and Retta. And if they hurt her, he'd take his time tearing them apart limb by limb.

He returned to the living room and paced the floor. He had time to devise a new plan but needed to remain calm.

Think.

The phone rang. Raheem.

"Hello?"

"Hey, glad I caught you," Raheem said. "I had a chance to look up the black car you sent me a photo of. Belongs to a man named Jeremiah Bivens. Get this, he's listed as Retta Sharp's attorney, but I can't find any evidence he has a law license or practiced anywhere. Even more interesting, he's been her so-called attorney on every single one of her cases."

"Her partner in crime and probably her lover."

"Right."

Hunter stopped pacing. "I have news for you. Jeremiah and Retta kidnapped Sable."

"What!"

"You heard me. I'm going to need your help getting her back."

Chapter Eleven

Maplewood Nature Preserve was located twenty-five minutes outside Hopevale and featured a number of amenities for active families—hiking trails, a lake and ponds, picnic tables, restrooms, a playground, a kids' obstacle course, and a bicycle trail. Because the preserve closed at seven, Hunter parked his car outside the gate and hopped the brick wall that denoted the property line on the eastern side.

He landed on his feet in the dirt and directed his gaze down the path. Tall trees with green, leafy branches stretched toward the night sky in the fading light.

"I'm in," he said in a low voice, solely for the two people listening—Raheem and Mouse. "Can you hear me?"

"Loud and clear," Raheem said. He had parked across the highway at a gas station. He gave Hunter a keychain equipped with a tracker and audio recorder, but the limited range meant he couldn't remain too far away. He would follow in a few minutes on foot.

"Got you," Mouse said, sounding slightly winded. She had

entered the preserve on foot from the north end and monitored his location from a handheld device. "You're nuts for meeting these people unarmed. You don't even know how many there are."

"That's why you're here."

"Lucky for you I was free," she quipped.

Hunter smiled, silently acknowledging the truth of her words. Mouse was one of the country's best long-range shooters Americans had never heard of, able to hit targets up to two miles away. She wouldn't be anywhere near that far away if she could get in the right position.

"I'm on the move," Hunter said.

He didn't know where Retta and Jeremiah were or if they had accomplices, so he simply followed the path, on alert for unusual movement in the woods. He'd walked about a quarter of a mile when a snapping twig brought him to a full stop. A man's form emerged from the trees, and when he came fully into view, Hunter couldn't believe his eyes.

"Detective Frank, you son of a bitch."

The detective held a gun in front of him as he strolled toward Hunter.

"Were you involved from the beginning?" Hunter asked.

"No, but Retta and Jeremiah made me an offer I couldn't refuse." He shrugged. "Are you armed?"

"I was told not to bring a weapon."

"But are you armed?"

"No. Want to frisk me?" Hunter stretched his arms on either side of his torso.

Detective Frank hesitated, then he shook his head. "Not here. Keep moving, straight ahead."

Hunter did as instructed. Dirt and rocks crunched under his feet. "How much farther?"

"Don't worry about that. I'll let you know when you need to stop."

They walked for another five minutes and came to a clearing at a pond. Moonlight reflected on the still surface, and picnic tables with benches sat at various spots along the grassy bank.

Like an apparition, Jeremiah stepped out from the trees and came toward them. He stood a few feet behind the cop.

"Where is she?" Hunter demanded.

Retta appeared holding a gun. She pushed Sable ahead of her, hands bound together by zip ties in front of her.

Relief loosened the tightness in Hunter's muscles.

"Hello again," Retta said.

Her pale skin seemed to glow in the dim light, and her demeanor had changed. The frightened, abused wife persona was gone, replaced by a confident woman with a cocky tilt to her head.

"You okay, babe?" Hunter asked Sable.

She nodded. "Better now that you're here."

"Did you pat him down for weapons?" Jeremiah asked Detective Frank.

"I didn't want to risk it back there on my own. Arms up," he said to Hunter.

Hunter lifted his hands and widened his stance. As the detective approached, he angled his head to get a better look at Sable. Despite the limited light, he noticed discoloration on her cheek.

"What happened to your face?"

"I—"

"We got into a little scuffle back at the house," Jeremiah interjected.

"He *hit* you?" Hunter demanded, incredulous.

Sable nodded.

His blood pressure spiked. This motherfu—

He locked eyes with Jeremiah as raw fury scorched his blood. "You must be out of your fucking mind."

"What are you going to do about it?"

Hunter calmed his breathing and bit his bottom lip. Then he chuckled, curling his fingers into fists. "I'm gonna break your jaw," he said, keeping his voice low and lethal.

"Sure you will," the other man taunted.

Hunter stared at him as Detective Frank gingerly patted from his thigh to his ankle.

"You're not very smart, coming out here all alone," Retta said.

"Who says I'm alone? Maybe I brought a sniper with me." Hunter sent a silent message to Sable with his eyes and saw the moment realization hit her. She knew Mouse was a sniper.

Retta looked around nervously.

"You'll never get away with this," Hunter said to bring her attention back to him.

"We already have," Retta said.

"You killed your husband in cold blood. You really think you can just walk away?"

Retta laughed. "You underestimate how good we are." Her narcissism was on full display.

"No weapons. This is the only thing I found on him." The detective held up the keychain with three keys on it. He stepped back from Hunter.

Hunter heard Mouse in his ear. "I'm in position but need to calibrate my scope."

"Oh, I know how good you are," Hunter continued. "I know you murdered your other three spouses and Jeremiah has been your accomplice the entire time."

"Then you know we'll get away with it, like we did before. Clyde is no different."

"You have no regret for murdering your previous spouses?"

Retta let out a brief laugh. "Why should I? I never loved them, and I earned every dime. Now, where's the Liberty Head coin?"

"In a safe place. I'll give you the nickel when you let Sable go," Hunter said.

"You're not in charge here!" Retta snapped.

"Forgive me if I'm a little concerned that you'll kill us once you get the coin. The remote location is a dead giveaway."

"If you don't give me the coin by the time I count to three, I'm going to shoot her." Retta jabbed the gun barrel into Sable's side, and she let out a moan of pain.

"One... two..."

Hunter's hand shot up. "Wait! It's in my shoe."

"Take it out!" Retta snarled.

"Don't hurt her." Hunter moved slowly, bending to his shoe.

"Watch him," Jeremiah warned.

Detective Frank stood with his feet shoulder width apart and kept his weapon trained on Hunter.

"I'm in position," Mouse said in Hunter's ear.

He lifted a penny from under the tongue of his shoe. It was the same coppery color as the Liberty Head nickel, and in the darkness, they wouldn't be able to tell the difference.

"Here you go." He tossed the coin at Retta.

Her mouth fell open on a gasp. At the same time, Sable flung herself to the ground, and the distant sound of a gunshot pierced the night. Retta cried out as her body twisted one hundred and eighty degrees before she collapsed to the ground on her back, bleeding from her right shoulder.

From the corner of his eye, Hunter saw Raheem race from between the trees, but he focused on Detective Frank, who had turned completely in Retta's direction. He tackled him from behind. The older man grunted as he hit the grass, but he held onto his gun. His elbow connected with Hunter's torso, but the blow only grazed his ribs. Raising onto his knees, Hunter pinned the detective's gun hand to the ground and punched him hard in the back of the head.

He only needed to hit him once. The dangerous blow could cause spinal injury and brain damage. The detective's body went limp and his head fell into the dirt.

"I don't have a shot! He's getting away!" Mouse yelled in Hunter's ear.

Jeremiah scrambled across the ground like the snake he was and hopped to his feet at the tree line. Hunter snatched up the detective's gun and aimed, but Jeremiah disappeared into the trees.

"Shit." Hunter lowered the weapon.

"You shot me. You shot me," Retta sobbed, while Raheem tied her hands behind her back.

"Quit your whining," his friend said.

Hunter hurried over to Sable, who remained seated on the ground. "You okay?'

"Yes. Go. He's getting away!"

He grasped the back of her head and gave her a quick kiss before he took off into the woods after Jeremiah.

Chapter Twelve

I t was hard as hell to see with the trees cutting off most of the limited natural light. But Hunter moved swiftly, racing in the general direction he saw Jeremiah run in, swiping at the underbrush to protect his face. His long strides ate up the earth, his breaths and the steady slap of his feet hitting the earth competing with the sounds of nature's night-time critters.

Hunter hopped over a large rock, and as he passed between two particularly wide tree trunks, he lost his footing. With a low grunt, he slid down an embankment. He grasped onto a bush to keep from tumbling deeper into the ditch, but doing so forced him to release the gun, which slid away into the dark.

He swore softly but pressed his feet into the loose earth and shoved himself back onto level ground. Standing still, chest heaving, he paid attention to his surroundings and forced himself to listen, as he had been trained to do. Then he heard the sound he had been searching for.

He took off to the left and moved swiftly, pushing away

branches and hopping over a large root. Eventually, he burst out of the line of trees and watched as Jeremiah landed on the other side of a wire fence. He raced toward a helicopter in the open field.

No, no. Hunter couldn't let him get away.

"Let's go!" Jeremiah screamed at the pilot.

With a burst of energy, Hunter ran toward the fence, scaled it in seconds, and dropped to the other side.

The helicopter rotors started turning.

Hunter ran as fast as he could, arms and legs pumping. Jeremiah leaped through the open door, and the helicopter slowly lifted from the ground. The rotors kicked up dust and flung hot air into Hunter's face. In one last act of desperation, he shot his body upward, grabbing onto the landing skids.

The chopper tilted sideways under the sudden weight but then stabilized. As they climbed higher, warm air swept over Hunter's skin. He hung on, feet dangling as they climbed higher off the ground.

Jeremiah gaped at him in disbelief, holding the back of the pilot's seat to stay steady.

"Do you ever give up?" he yelled.

"Never," Hunter yelled back.

Jeremiah's nostrils flared, and he eased toward the open door. The wind whipped his dark hair across his forehead, and his eyes filled with malicious intent.

Hunter flung one leg up and over the landing gear. The move clearly threatened Jeremiah, because he took the risky move of kicking at Hunter's shoulder. Hunter winced beneath the pain but quickly recovered and grabbed Jeremiah's foot with one hand. The fake attorney cried out in panic and stumbled back, losing his shoe in the process. His retreat was the opening Hunter needed. He tossed away the shoe and used brute strength and sheer will to haul himself into the chopper.

Jeremiah's eyes widened. He made a valiant effort to defend himself with a wild swing, but Hunter easily blocked the blow with his forearm in the confined space and followed with a sharp uppercut that made Jeremiah's head bounce against the ceiling, surely rattling his brain inside his skull. Two jabs to the chest, knocked the air from Jeremiah's lungs, and then a left and a right hook to either side of his face finished him off. He collapsed in the seat, bleeding from his mouth, face twisted from a broken jaw.

Hunter clutched a handful of his hair and forced Jeremiah to look him in the eye. "That's for putting your hands on my woman."

Hunter hit him in the middle of the forehead, and he slumped against the wall, semi-conscious.

Head bent against the low ceiling, Hunter tapped the pilot on the shoulder.

"Take us down. Now."

The pilot nervously nodded and turned the bird into a downward descent.

*   *   *

The police arrived in the clearing and took the pilot and Jeremiah into custody. Raheem had shared with other officers the incriminating recording of Retta admitting to killing her wife and husbands. That recorded evidence earned her and Detective Frank a police escort to the hospital. Raheem, Mouse, and Sable were all waiting on Hunter now.

He walked out of the woods with sore knuckles, scratches on his face and hands, but otherwise in good shape. Mouse and Sable sat atop one of the picnic tables with their feet resting on the bench. Raheem paced in front of them. The minute he saw Hunter, he stopped pacing.

Sable looked over her shoulder and let out a squeal of delight. She jumped off the table and ran to Hunter, leaping into his arms and wrapping her arms and legs around his waist.

He caught her with a husky laugh. "Hey, you," he said, cradling her bottom in his hands.

He was still upset by the sight of her red, bruised cheek but was satisfied he'd made Jeremiah pay for having the audacity to put a hand on her.

"Hey, yourself. Looks like you had a rough time." She brushed dirt off the front of his shirt.

"Nothing I couldn't handle."

Sable planted her mouth against his, sucking on his bottom lip and moaning with pleasure. His body hardened at her enthusiastic greeting.

"Good to see you too," he said with a grin.

She giggled and rested her soft cheek against his. "Glad it's over."

"Me too. You sure have a knack for attracting trouble."

Sable shot him a look. "Me? You're the one who brought me to Hopevale, a quiet little Georgia town, allegedly."

He chuckled. "Hopefully this will be the last time you ever have to experience anything like this."

Sable sighed and rested her forehead against his.

"You okay?" he asked quietly.

"Mhmm. I'm okay."

"Guys, I hate to break up your little reunion, but can we get out of here?" Mouse asked.

Sable lowered to her feet and they strolled over to the other two.

"Thanks a lot, Mouse. You came through, like always." Hunter pulled his petite friend into a side hug.

"No problem."

"Raheem, thanks, man." He gave Raheem some dap.

"Any time. Let's get out of here."

Raheem led the way back down the path, with Mouse in the middle, and Hunter and Sable holding hands, pulling up the rear.

Chapter Thirteen

A small crowd assembled in front of Sable's Treasures, Antiques & Collectibles for the ribbon-cutting. Gold and black balloons created a festive atmosphere on either side of the front of the store. In addition to spectators, the group included a councilwoman, a cameraman and reporter from a locally-produced YouTube news channel, and a writer for the events section of the *Hopevale Daily*.

Sable wore heels and a tailored green dress that brought out the green in her hazel eyes, and her hair parted on the side and cascading past her shoulders in waves. Excitement coursed through her veins as she listened to the councilwoman introduce her and her business as the latest addition to the downtown landscape of the small community. As the politician spoke into the microphone, an interpreter signed the words a few feet away—something Sable had insisted on since she was ever conscious of the hearing impaired because of her daughter Avril. Steadfast and supportive, Hunter watched from the back of the group, a faint smile on his face.

During the past week, their lives settled into normalcy. The

Liberty Head coin had been returned to Clyde's family and Retta, Jeremiah, and Detective Frank were in police custody. After such a tumultuous period, Sable was grateful to be standing in front of her store. She and Hunter worked hard to prepare for the opening, and her dream had come true. She couldn't have done it without his help.

The councilwoman said Sable's name, her cue to step forward and give a short speech before cutting the ribbon. She introduced herself, stated the type of items she would be selling, and then invited everyone inside to view the store. She then turned and used the scissors to cut the gold ribbon across the door. The group cheered and clapped and then shuffled through the entrance.

The shelves contained merchandise like dainty figurines, vintage hair brushes, and vases from decades ago. A grandfather clock stood like a sentry against one wall, while the glass display under the cash register presented a collection of rare coins and wartime medals for the collector with more money to spend.

Sable didn't have staff yet. She planned to hire someone once business picked up, but for now the store would be open at eleven in the morning and close at five-thirty Tuesday through Saturday. For today's event, Hunter would man the register while she circulated amongst the customers, answering questions and explaining the historical significance of various pieces.

By the time five-thirty rolled around, she guessed she'd had a robust sales day. When she finally closed the door and locked it, she leaned back and released a satisfied sigh. Then she burst into happy laughter.

"Did that really just happen?" Sable asked Hunter.

Behind the counter, he nodded. "That really happened. Day one of opening your store, and you had a great sales day."

Sable kicked off her shoes and pranced over to the register. "How did we do?"

Hunter ran the sales tape and she gasped.

"I can't believe it," she said. They'd sold in the low four digits.

"Not too bad," Hunter said, nodding his head.

She was not naïve enough to think her sales would be that high every day, but she was excited by the interest from the patrons and hoped the publicity and customers generated good word-of-mouth.

"And thirty-six people signed up for your newsletter list," Hunter added, showing her the sign-up sheet.

"Amazing. I couldn't have done it without you."

"Sure you could have, but it wouldn't have been as much fun."

He slipped his arms around her waist and she flung her arms around his neck.

"True," she admitted.

Hunter gazed down at her. "I'm proud of you. You've worked really hard to get to this point, and you deserve every success. Can't wait to see how much your business is going to grow."

"I've already been thinking about how I could attract customers from Atlanta and the surrounding towns. So many ideas are buzzing in my head."

"Can we put those ideas on hold until after dinner?"

"Is my baby hungry?" she teased.

"Starving."

Sable laughed and patted his chest. "Then let's get you fed. Where do you want to eat?"

Hunter pulled the keys from his pocket. "Let's drive to Atlanta and have dinner."

"I like that idea. Do you have someplace in mind?" Sable

lifted her purse onto her shoulder.

"There's this restaurant named Kayak. They have a little bit of everything—seafood, steaks, that kind of thing."

"Ooh, sounds fancy. We're eating good tonight."

"Tonight's a special night. We're celebrating the opening of Sable's Treasures, Antiques & Collectibles."

"I like the sound of that. Thank you so much for your help." She raised onto her toes and gave Hunter a quick kiss.

"I need to go home and change, then we can head out."

"Is my dress okay?" Sable smoothed a hand down her hips.

His eyes warmed with a spark of desire as they drifted over her figure. "Your whole outfit is perfect. You look beautiful. Ready?"

"Ready."

After a quick stop at home, they took the long drive to Kayak. The upscale restaurant was tucked away behind one of the city's most exclusive neighborhoods. When they arrived, the host escorted them through the main dining room to the glass-enclosed sunroom where they could look out at a narrow section of the Chattahoochee River trickling by and sparkling under the lights strung through the trees.

Sable glanced around at the other tables, occupied mostly by couples and foursomes. "This is so nice. Good choice."

He grinned at her and then lowered his eyes to the menu.

Handsome as always, Hunter wore a black dress shirt and gray slacks. She'd chickened out of bringing up the marriage conversation during the busy period of prepping for the store opening, and now was not a good time. But she planned to broach the topic in the next day or two.

They ordered dinner and started with the apple and radicchio salad. For an entree, Sable chose the salmon and Hunter the roasted chicken with root vegetables. Though she insisted she didn't have room for dessert, she couldn't resist the pumpkin panna cotta with fresh cream. Hunter ate a truffle cake and finished off her panna cotta when she slid the small plate over to him.

"Everything was delicious." Stuffed and happy, Sable sighed. The day couldn't have gone better.

"Did you talk to Avril today?" Hunter placed a credit card into the bill folder and slid it to the edge of the table. The waiter glided by and picked it up with one smooth move.

"I did. She was excited when I told her the opening went well, and I promised to send her the YouTube video when I get the link. I sent her the photo you took of me." She wrinkled her nose.

He reached for her hand on the table. "You looked fine."

"Well, I do appreciate you getting my good side."

"Yes, I learned my lesson after you chewed me out."

"I did *not* chew you out."

"Your exact words were, 'What is this? Please tell me you can do better than this.' Did I misquote you?" He arched an eyebrow, amusement filling his gray eyes.

"Nooo," Sable reluctantly admitted. "But let's be real, I couldn't share that photo on Instagram."

"Here we go."

He moved to release her hand, but she grasped him tight.

"I'm just saying. You know I'm right."

"Yes, dear," he said, sounding exhausted.

"Hunter! Don't do that."

He chuckled and lifted her knuckles to his lips. "I've always been told, if you want peace in your home, pretend your woman is always right."

"*Pretend.* Oh. That's nice."

Sable tried to tug away her hand, but this time he held on.

His eyes softened with humor but also affection. "I love you so much."

Her heart stopped beating for a second. He'd expressed his love for her in the past, but sitting in this fine dining restaurant and having him look so intently at her somehow made the words more powerful. She was so lucky not only to have Hunter, but that he openly shared his feelings.

Sable teared up and swallowed the lump in her throat. "Love you too."

The waiter arrived with the receipt, and after Hunter signed it, he stood. Taking Sable's hand and pulling her to her feet, he said, "Let's go outside and walk around the grounds for a bit. Walk off some of this food."

Hand in hand, they strolled onto the property, along the cobblestone pathway that led to a small bridge. On the way, they passed another couple making out under a tree. They glanced at each other and smiled, understanding how the need to be affectionate could overcome the need for propriety.

They crossed a small, low bridge to another section of the grounds, with only glimpses of the restaurant behind them. For the most part, they were alone in the night, with the chirp of crickets blending with the sound of leaves rustling in the gentle breeze.

"They have a koi pond out here," Hunter said, pointing.

Sable left him behind and walked over to the pond. "How did you know about this?"

Lights hung from the tree branches and illuminated the colorful fish swimming back and forth in the water.

"I came out here once before and looked around. The host said once a week they have musicians playing music on the grounds."

"That would be nice, to come back one day and listen to the musicians. We should—"

Her sentence broke off on a gasp the minute she turned to face Hunter.

Chapter Fourteen

D own on one knee, Hunter gazed up at the woman he loved. The woman he wanted to spend the rest of his life with.

He'd gone over proposal scenarios in his head multiple times and thought about popping the question quietly and at home, then reconsidered because he wanted to make the event more special. But a big production didn't appeal to him. He didn't want to make a spectacle of them, nor did he—deep, deep down—want to risk asking Sable to marry him in front of others, with the off chance she might say *No*.

So here he was after a drive into the city and an expensive dinner at a fine-dining restaurant. In his palm sat a black box with a vintage engagement ring. The Art Deco design, circa 1930s, was centered with one brilliant cut diamond accented with eighteen round, single cut diamonds on a platinum band. Down on one knee, heart in his throat, he hoped she liked the ring he had chosen and hoped, more than anything, the expression of shock on her face didn't mean he'd gotten her thoughts on marriage wrong.

"I..." Hunter cleared his throat. "I had this long speech planned, but I don't want to say any of it. I just want you to know that I love you so much, Sable. When Retta and Jeremiah took you away from me, my heart hurt so much I thought I'd die from the fear of losing you. That's it. I love you and want to spend the rest of my life with you. Will you marry me?" He held his breath.

Her lips expanded into a smile of pure happiness. "Yes! I *will* marry you."

As a tear streamed down her left cheek, Hunter slipped the ring on her trembling finger. Then he stood and pulled her into a hug. Relieved. Ecstatic. Overwhelmed by a gamut of emotions. His life was finally complete. Everything he'd been missing was right here in his arms.

"Love you, babe," Hunter whispered, kissing her tear-damp cheek.

She cradled his face in her hands. "Thank you. For loving me and my daughter and for just being you. Love you."

They kissed and he pulled her close, arms tight around her back. He kissed behind her ear and the scented hollow of her neck. Running his hands down the roundness of her bottom, he squeezed a handful of ass and groaned.

"Let's go home."

"Okay," Sable whispered against his mouth, flicking her tongue along his lower lip before they withdrew from each other.

They hurried around the side of the building to the car.

* * *

They arrived at home in record time.

At the staircase leading to the second floor, Hunter grabbed Sable from behind and brushed aside her curtain of hair. Kissing her neck, he tugged down the zipper of her dress. She arched her back and let her bottom bump against his pelvis. The soft cushion of her ass made his loins tingle and he became harder, as if he hadn't been hard the entire drive from Atlanta.

She turned to face him, biting her bottom lip. That little bite was so damn sexy. Grabbing the front of his shirt, she walked backwards and pulled him up the stairs with sultry, inviting eyes. When she looked at him like that—like a little sex kitten—she could lead him into a fiery pit and he'd happily accept the burns.

Inside the bedroom, he undressed her with a quickness by pushing her unzipped dress down her arms to the floor and peeling off her lingerie. He stripped off his own clothes and then sat on the bed. Hand on her waist, he pulled her between his legs and brought her tantalizing breasts within kissing distance.

But he licked her midriff first, his muscles tightening with anticipation at the sound of her sexy little moans. She cupped the back of his head in silent encouragement, and he dragged her onto his lap so that she straddled him with her knees on the bed.

Their kiss was hungry, their mouths and tongues slipping and sliding over each other. Hunter moved his lips lower, down her chin to the smooth line of her arched neck and her hands gripped the back of his head tighter. He smiled against her skin. Her throat was sensitive, so he spent a little more time there, nipping the delicate flesh with his teeth and drawing trembling sighs from the back of her throat.

Hunter dragged his hands over her soft skin—toned thighs, round hips, and higher to the twin prizes on her chest, her full breasts. He squeezed them together and dragged his stiff tongue over the tip of her left nipple. Closing his lips over the hard peak, he took pleasure in the sweetness of her skin and the way her moans became louder.

He eased her backward at an angle over his thighs and took his time on each breast. He loved on the soft mounds with his tongue and sucked on the tight chocolate nipples, using the edge of his teeth to drag against them until she tossed back her head and clutched at his short curls.

He loved when she lost control and gave herself over to pleasure and desire. Her responsiveness encouraged him to seek new ways to satisfy her sexual needs.

Sable's hips rocked against his hard dick, and the grinding movement dampened his hard shaft and caused a helpless groan to leave him.

"You want this dick now, don't you?" Hunter rasped.

"Please," she panted.

With one fluid movement, Hunter rose from the bed, and her legs locked around his waist. She showered soft kisses on his jaw and neck as he moved to the side of the bed. Placing her gently on the mattress, he pushed her legs apart and exposed her glistening sex to his hungry gaze. He could hardly wait to taste her. He could hardly wait to fill his mouth with her moist flesh.

Climbing onto the bed, he lowered his lips to the valley between her breasts. Her torso undulated off the bed as he kissed his way down her belly to the prize below. He stopped right at her pelvis and looked up between her legs. Her lips parted in anticipation, and her chest heaved with each deep inhale she took.

"Hunter..." Sable breathed his name like a prayer, her face pleading.

And who was he to deny her?

He grabbed her hips and roughly pulled her toward his mouth. She gasped, and as he pressed his face to her flesh, her head snapped back. He kissed and licked the swollen folds and sucked on her engorged clit.

She twisted on the bed, and the semi-dark room filled with the sound of her whimpering cries. Hunter smoothed his hands up her silky thighs which sandwiched his head, then lifted her legs onto his shoulders and continued to indulge his hunger. He was hard as a rock and so turned on. Her moans and feminine musk, and the taste of her juices on his tongue—all conspired to bring him dangerously close to exploding.

When he sealed his lips around her clit and flicked it with the tip of his tongue, the combination of sucking and stroking was Sable's undoing.

She cried out as an orgasm ravaged her body. But Hunter was a greedy son of a bitch, refusing to stop when he heard her cries of completion. He thrust his tongue deep and gently sucked her damp folds. Her thighs trembled around his ears as she gasped for air and clawed the bedsheets.

When he finally had enough, Hunter released her and lifted his head. On all fours, he licked his lips clean and captured every last bit of flavor. Mesmerized, he watched her pretty breasts rise and lower in an effort to catch her breath.

"You feel good, babe?" he whispered huskily.

A lazy smile curved her lips. "Yes. You always make me feel good."

Hunter lowered onto her body, and Sable welcomed him with open arms. She smoothed her hands down the base of his spine and sank her fingers into his buttocks when he pressed the tip of his penis at her entrance. Her hips lifted, and she took the initial thrust with a sharply indrawn breath. One hand on her left hip, Hunter withdrew then thrust in again. His body shuddered. She was so warm and wet.

Goddamn.

Every time he pulled back, Sable bowed her hips to meet

the subsequent push of his. Over and over until their rhythm increased to a frantic pace. Hunter clenched his jaw, barely managing to hold back so he could give her another orgasm. But it wasn't easy. His baby felt so good he was damn near losing his mind.

Their fingers locked together, and his gaze landed on the sparkling ring on her finger. Very soon she would be his. Permanently. The thought sent a shot of intense heat to his loins, and his hold on her tightened.

Mine. Mine.

The mattress groaned under the increasing speed of his thrusts, and her breasts jostled with each downward stroke.

Sable's cry as she fell over the edge made the skin on the back of his neck tingle. Chanting his name, she strained upward, pushing against his hips.

He fastened his lips to hers and her mouth opened into a hot, hungry kiss. As her muscles contracted around him, Hunter's control slipped. He grunted and his face contorted from utmost pleasure. Burying his nose in her scented neck, he squeezed his eyes shut as his warm cum shot into her core. He shuddered once, twice, under the force of his release.

Then he drew a deep breath and collapsed his weight on top of her.

Chapter Fifteen

Hunter checked the back door and windows downstairs before turning off the light in the kitchen. He padded barefoot and naked through the house to the front door with two protein bars in his hand. One wrapped, the other he'd already taken a bite from.

He checked the front door and then peered through the window. The street was quiet. No movement in the shadows, and Retta and Clyde's house was cloaked in darkness. After a while, he figured a real estate agent would place a *For Sale* sign in the yard, and he idly wondered who the new neighbors would be. Anyone would be an improvement on Retta, that's for sure.

He climbed the stairs to the bedroom. As soon as he slipped under the covers, Sable scooted over and flung an arm over his chest.

"Want a bite?" He offered the protein bar.

She bit off a piece and chewed. Hunter ate the rest and opened the second one.

Sable tucked her hair behind one ear. "How do you feel about kids?" she asked.

Chewing on a bite of the snack gave Hunter time to think. He couldn't believe they hadn't discussed children before he asked her to marry him. He had been so anxious to pop the question.

"You know I love Avril, but I would like to have a child of my own," he answered honestly. "Maybe two. How do you feel about that?"

"I would like to have two more."

"So we're on the same page?" That was certainly good news.

Sable nodded, grinning.

Hunter eased the sheet lower on her body and spread his fingers over her flat stomach. He smiled at the thought of Sable pregnant with their child.

"I'm going to be a dad," he whispered.

Except for his Cordoba teammates, he'd never had a family of his own, and until he met Sable hadn't considered "forever" with anyone. All that had changed. The thought of having his own family with little kids running around made him emotional.

"You won't be a father right away," Sable said in an amused tone. "I have to get off birth control, and then it could be months before I get pregnant."

Hunter snorted. "Months? You don't know my sperm. These guys are tenacious. They don't mess around."

"Oh really? Your sperm can defeat science?"

"I'm not gonna argue with you about facts."

Sable started laughing and shook her head.

Hunter broke the last of the bar into two parts and handed one to her.

After they finished eating, they settled lower in the bed, facing each other with their heads on one pillow.

Sable flung a leg over his thighs and closed her eyes. Eventually they would pull apart, but he liked the postcoital cuddling. He traced the curve of her eyebrow with the pad of his thumb.

"You know what I was thinking?" he asked in a quiet voice.

Sable opened her eyes. "What?"

"We should probably get a little more practice on this baby-making idea."

The corners of her lips eased higher, and her eyes turned sultry. "I think you're right. The more practice the better."

He laughed softly. God he loved this woman. "Once again, we're on the same page."

With languorous kisses and gentle caresses, they made love slowly, and their heated pants evolved into low groans. Her stroking hands turned the flesh between his thighs hard with desire, and his hands roamed over her body in slow motion, turning her nipples hard and making her wet as he fondled the cleft between her legs.

They came together again, their bodies joining into one. They rocked slowly at first, less hurried than the first time, using whisper-soft, affectionate kisses to convey their feelings for each other.

After Hunter came, mere seconds after Sable did, he rolled onto his back and dragged her with him.

He held her close for a very long time with her head nestled on his shoulder and her soft breasts flat on his chest. When he finally did move, he threaded his fingers through her fingers with the engagement ring and lifted her hand to kiss her knuckles.

Then he smiled.

When he asked Sable to move to Georgia to be with him,

he didn't know what the future would bring. He only knew he hated being apart from her and needed her near.

Now she was going to be his wife. They were going to have a family.

Even better days lay ahead.

The Royal Brides series

Read the Royal Brides series!

Princess of Zamibia (Royal Brides #1)

Prince Kofi wants his son, and he'll do whatever it takes to bring his heir back to Zamibia, even if it means marrying the woman he believes betrayed him.

Princess of Estoria (Royal Brides #2)

Prince Andres is incapable of taking no for an answer. The playboy prince has set his sights on Angela, and neither the vastness of the ocean nor the distance of continents will keep him away. But when reality steps in, he's forced to make a tough decision that could change the course of history. (Inspired by current events.)

Queen of Barrakesch (Royal Brides #3)

To become king, Prince Wasim al-Hassan agrees to a fake engagement with his friend, Imani. But when the marriage must proceed as planned, Imani fights to keep the ultimate secret—that she is madly in love with him.

The Cordoba Agency series

Read The Cordoba Agency series!

Until Now (The Cordoba Agency #1)

For Cruz Cordoba, a simple off-the-books assignment becomes a race of life and death.

Until Death (The Cordoba Agency #2)

The best laid plans can still go awry . . . in the most terrifying way. Read the exciting conclusion to Cruz and Shanice's love story.

Heart Stealer (The Cordoba Agency #3)

Katherine was older, sophisticated, and years ago she broke Raheem's heart. Now he must keep her alive and his desire in check. Easier said than done.

Almost Perfect (The Cordoba Agency #4)

A cat burglar and an assassin run for their lives across Paris—and try not to get distracted by the sizzling attraction between them.

* * *

Audiobook samples, free short stories, and the full catalogue of books are available at www.delaneydiamond.com.

About the Author

Delaney Diamond is the USA Today Bestselling Author of sensual and passionate romance novels. She reads romance novels, mysteries, thrillers, and a fair amount of nonfiction. When she's not busy reading or writing, she's in the kitchen trying out new recipes, dining at one of her favorite restaurants, or traveling to an interesting locale.

Enjoy free reads and the first chapter of all her novels on her website. Join her mailing list to get sneak peeks, notices of sale prices, and find out about new releases.

Join her mailing list
www.delaneydiamond.com

facebook.com/DelaneyDiamond

twitter.com/DelaneyDiamond

bookbub.com/authors/delaney-diamond

pinterest.com/delaneydiamond

goodreads.com/delaney_diamond

* 9 7 8 1 9 4 6 3 0 2 7 1 7 *